Murder on Oregon's Coast Highway - 1961

By Joe R. Blakely

Author of

*The Bellfountain Giant Killers, Lifting Oregon Out of the Mud,
Oswald West Governor of Oregon 1911-1915, et al.*

First Edition, 2017

Cover photo:

Front cover: Photograph of Oregon's Coast Highway
near Cape Sebastian, circa 1961, courtesy of the
Oregon Department of Transportation.
Back cover: Photograph of Thomas Creek Bridge,
circa 1962, and a 1959 map of Oregon, courtesy of the
Oregon Department of Transportation

Published by

Groundwaters Publishing, LLC
P.O. Box 50, Lorane, Oregon 97451
http://www.groundwaterspublishing.com

ISBN-13: 978-1977617132
ISBN-10: 1977617131

Dedication

I dedicate this book to the Governors, Legislators, and concerned citizens who, with foresight and courage, preserved Oregon's beaches and rugged coastline for all to enjoy.

Tribute to the Roosevelt Highway
circa 1920s

Like a silver thread I wind my
Way,

through forests, vales and hills:

By sparkling brooks of water clear;
O'er mountain grades and fills...
My course is laid through grandest
Views
Of mountain crest and valley
Stream.

Where sweetest native flowers
Bloom,
And scenic beauty rules supreme.

— Author unknown

Chapter One

"Charley, I want you to take a two-week vacation, get out of town for a while," said Bruce Zeler, editor of the Oregonian. Zeler's desk separated the men. With his index finger Charley pushed back the large, dark rimmed glasses that had slipped down his nose. He was not sure he wanted to leave town.

"We're getting phone calls hourly, and the letters to the editor are stacking up. Look at my desk!" Bruce Zeler threw his big hairy hands in the air. "All these letters were written in response to your editorials. It took nerve for you to expose the prostitution operation. Now the crooks and pimps are calling with death threats. Charley, they want to kill you too. Do you hear me?"

"We can't let them scare us into silence," Charley said. "It's people like them who raped and killed my mother. They shot my father. I won't stop writing about them. My father never did and I won't either. I want these thugs behind bars or dead. Bruce, we got them on the run, looking over their shoulder. They're scared."

Bruce rolled his chair around the corner of his desk, coming face to face with Charley. Their noses almost touched. Bruce's desk fan whirred, rustling papers. The breeze blew across Charley's furrowed brow. Bruce's brown hair fluttered and his brown, forty-five-year-old eyes squinted as they stared down blue ones.

"They're not scared. The police are their paid henchmen. Your life isn't worth a plug of tobacco. Your stories are selling papers. Our owners are profiting. But you're the one sticking his neck out. I don't want to lose the best writer I ever had." Sweat beaded on Bruce's large forehead. His hand came thundering down on his desk. "Damn it, why is it that newspapers have to expose corruption?"

Bruce rolled his chair back around his cluttered desk. His half-framed reading glasses clung to the tip of his nose. He looked over the lenses at his star reporter, only 24 years old, curly red hair, thin, and six feet tall. His big glasses made him look boyish. Bruce didn't want him hurt. "Maybe we should ease up on them. Give 'em a break."

"No! Right now, seated at my desk, I've got a young lady who says she can tell me who the crime boss is. I can't stop now."

"It might be a set up."

Charley glanced around the office. Hanging on the walls were photographs of past sensational front-page stories. Two of them had been written by his father. A big fluorescent light hung overhead. Charley remembered what his father had once said. "Son, when you write stories about people you must be dead sure your sources are correct. Every statement must be double-and triple-checked. You don't ever want to incriminate the wrong person."

"Maybe you should step back," Bruce said. "Take on another assignment, get out of town, and get your thoughts together. Let the thugs sweat a while. Then come back in two weeks and hit them with everything you got."

Charley also remembered his father saying, "When you're on a crusade it's important you have your thoughts lined up. Don't be impulsive. Let the yeast rise. When you're sure of its consistency, attack."

Charley wondered if his story had reached that point yet. Maybe not. Was he ready to stake his reputation on the statements of one girl? "Listen to your editor," his father had said.

The door behind him popped open and a clerk's face poked in. "The advertising editor wants to meet with you," she said.

"I'll be right there," Bruce said.

"Listen Charley, take a two-week paid vacation down the Oregon coast. Write some stories about businesses, resorts, beaches, parks and people. Anything you think interesting. Oregon's coast is filled with good stories. I'm especially interested in the highway they're building near Brookings. I've heard it's Oregon's biggest road project ever. Find out about it. Portlanders want to know. When you come back we'll print your stories. Then we'll expose the racketeers. What do you say?"

Charley nodded. "I'll leave tomorrow morning."

Chapter Two

Seated next to Charley's desk was a young woman perhaps his own age. Blond hair tumbled off her head to rest on her shoulders. She wore a blue floral dress with a blue belt around her thin waist. Blue eyes flashed under blond eyebrows and a gently curved brow. Her clenched mouth betrayed tenseness. Above that was a slightly upturned nose. When she saw Charley coming she looked momentarily down and her hand swept back a lock of blond hair. When she looked up the tips of her lips quivered ever so slightly. Her wispy lean body practically floated on the chair. Her cheeks were damp. Charley thought she was so pretty she could be a model for a fashion magazine. In the large room other male reporters were typing articles and doing their best to keep from staring at her.

"You must be April Lewis?"

"Yes."

"I think we need some privacy for this meeting. You're creating quite a stir," Charley said, pushing his glasses back.

"I didn't mean to."

"Yes I know. This may not be the best place. I know of a café not far from here. We can have coffee and you can tell me, confidentially, what you know. I am very interested. Would that be suitable to you?"

"Okay, I guess."

Eyes followed them as they walked out the door to the elevator.

Five stories down they exited the elevator and walked into a big lobby. It was five p.m. The lobby was crowded with people leaving for the day. They managed their way into the revolving glass exit door. A couple of laughing teens pushed on the glass behind them, knocking April forward. She had to clutch onto Charley to keep from falling. They stumbled out onto the sidewalk, and were then jostled around by picketers holding signs: "The Oregonian has UNFAIR LABOR PRACTICES" and "We want our jobs back." Charley and April worked their way through them. The sidewalk became less crowded.

"This way," Charley said.

"Watch out!" April shouted. "Those two men…"

Charley was knocked off his feet from an unexpected shoulder to his chest. His glasses flew off and skidded along the sidewalk. As he lay there the man tried to kick him in the face. Charley was able to grab the foot and twisted it with all his strength. The man screamed and his knee almost snapped. He curled in pain, falling to the concrete.

When Charley looked for April she was being dragged to a parked car. He scrambled to his feet and raced after her. April was resisting, but was being overpowered by a huge brute. The door to the vehicle swung open. Charley flew through the air slamming his shoulder against the man's shin. The man fell backwards against the car. The jolt caused him to let go of April. He scrambled upright and kicked Charley in the face. Blood ran from Charley's nose. The thug had enough time to climb into the back seat of the parked car. The door slammed and he roared off.

Charley lay on the ground, bleeding from his mouth and nose. By this time April had managed to get up. She saw Charley's glasses on the sidewalk and quickly retrieved them.

"Here," she said.

Charley put them on. He slowly pushed himself to his feet. "Where's that other guy who knocked me down?"

"I don't know," said April.

When they looked back at the Oregonian building all they could see were the picketers with their signs.

"Are you okay?" Charley said.

"Yes. I'll be okay. Just a few scratches."

"You're stronger than you look. We need to talk. Let's get my car." Holding his handkerchief to his nose, he led April to where his car was parked a few blocks away.

"Thank you for saving me from those bullies," April said. She was still shaking.

Charley nodded. "Here's my car."

April's eyes flew open. "Nice car!" The two-door Chevrolet Bel Air convertible stood out like a red apple in a black-and-white photograph. Charley opened the passenger door to let April in. Then he walked around to the other side.

"Where are we going?" she asked.

"To the park under the St. John's Bridge." He drove through heavy traffic, heading toward the Willamette River and the bridge crossing. Soon they reached the towering bridge and crossed to the east side.

"We have some bridges like this in the southern part of the state," April said. "Not quite as old or elegant. We have the Rogue River Bridge at Gold Beach and the McCullough Bridge at Coos Bay. How is your nose doing?"

"I think the bleeding has almost stopped." He removed the handkerchief that he had held against his nose.

"Charley, I'm really scared."

"I know, I am too." Charley parked the car where they could see the St. John's Bridge spanning the Willamette River. "No matter how vicious they are we can't let them scare us. We have to stand up to them."

"Charley, I want to help you, but I'm not as brave as you. I don't want to get killed."

"I don't blame you. Most people are afraid to come forward. These men ruthlessly abuse women and murder those who try to stop them. But I'm beginning to unravel their crimes. After what happened today, I've got a feeling you're already involved. Do you have information that might help me?"

"I feel certain I have."

"That's why they were trying to kidnap you."

April pulled down the visor and adjusted it to block the sun. Then she moved a little closer to Charley on the vinyl seat. "I'm from Brookings on the Southern Oregon coast. I grew up there and always wanted to be an elementary school teacher. After high school I went to the University of Oregon and got my certificate to teach. Last September I started teaching in a Portland school."

"What grade do you teach?"

"Second grade. As soon as the school year ended I began making preparations to go home and see my parents. That's when all the trouble started."

"What trouble?"

"The mother of one of my students is a prostitute. She's been trying desperately to get out of that life, without much success. She lacks self confidence, and has no money. Her husband beats her regularly and demands that she work the streets as a whore.

"What is the mother's name?"

"Monica Taylor. On our second parent conference about her son, her husband came with her. She introduced him as Robert Taylor. I'll never forget him."

"What did he look like? He might be the ringleader I've been looking for."

"He was about your height but with black hair, a dark complexion, and what looked like dark brown eyes— almost black. He looked limber for his age, thin, and about forty-five. He seemed real fidgety as if he would explode any minute. He kept looking nervously around the room. He told the child's mother to hurry up.

I noticed she had some bruises on her arms and face."

"What did you say to him?"

"I told him that their son, Harry, was very disruptive. If it continued I'd have to report his behavior to my principal. That's when Robert erupted.

"He shouted at me, 'I'll report you to your principal. You're not doing your job. You're suppose to control my son, understand?'"

At this point April's eyes narrowed. Charley could see the fear in them. "Robert's hands flew wildly as he talked. Again and again he blamed me for his son's behavior. I was afraid he'd hit me. As they were leaving the conference, Robert pushed the mother and child out of the room. He stayed behind and said, 'Don't report my son to your principal.' He gave me a card with his phone number on it. 'Any more trouble with Harry you call me first or you'll be risking more then you can imagine.' He gave me an evil look.

"That's when I told him to leave: I was so mad that I walked to the classroom door and opened it. As soon as he was gone, I slammed and locked the door."

"You were brave to talk like that to such a dangerous man. Robert reminds me of… no, that couldn't be." Charley looked down.

"What are you talking about?"

Charley swabbed the last drops from his bleeding nose, and then looked out the window.

"What is it, Charley?"

"My parents were killed twelve years ago. My father was a journalist too. He had fought against corruption in Portland. One night after I had gone to bed, I heard noises from our living room. I opened my bedroom door a crack and saw the attack."

Charley covered his eyes. After a pause he continued. "My father was shot in the forehead at point blank range. The man in charge was just like the man you described, a menacing dark-complexioned thug. My mother attacked him with her fists. The man caught her by the arm and dragged her to his two accomplices. They raped her on our couch and then suffocated her with a sofa pillow. I saw the two men run out the front door." Charley choked up. He used the handkerchief to wipe his eyes.

"Their leader was the last to leave. He paused at the door and looked back. He must have seen my bedroom door ajar, but since it was dark he couldn't see me inside. But I could see him. One of his men called out, 'Hurry up Bob,' I held my breath until he left. April, I wonder if Mr. Taylor might be the same man."

"It's possible. Is that why you write your newspaper articles?"

"I guess my articles take up the battle where my father left off. Do you still have Taylor's card?"

April opened her purse and rummaged through it. "Here it is." She handed it to Charley. "When my principal heard the story he talked to the parents. After that, I started getting obscene phone calls and threats on my life. I reported it to the police but didn't hear back from them. That's when I decided to call you."

Chapter Three

"**D**id anyone get your license plate number?" Robert Taylor asked, smoke curling from his mouth. He sat at the desk in his palatial suite on the Damien Hotel's tenth floor.

"Our license plate was covered, boss," Sam said. "There was a lot of commotion with the picketers and all. I don't think we were even noticed. If that damn newspaperman hadn't been there I know we'd of bagged her. Afterwards we drove straight back to the hotel."

"I should have taken care of Charley Norman years ago," Robert said. "I knew he was watching from that bedroom." Robert held his cigarette with two yellow stained fingers and sucked in. When he exhaled he said, "We'll just have to take care of him now, eh boys?"

Sam nodded his bald head, rubbed his right hand over it, and smiled. The other henchman, Denton, had gray hair that flopped as he nodded. They looked like two different kinds of obedient dogs. Sam was built like a pit bull. Denton was thin and nervous like a chihuahua. Both men were glad to do anything Robert asked. He paid them well and, with prostitutes nearby—well, they loved the benefits.

They also knew that if they didn't call Robert "boss," he would fly into a rage. They made sure to answer all questions with "Yes, boss." They didn't want to be replaced.

Killing came easy to Robert, like paring an apple. He showed no emotion, no remorse for his crimes. His face was calm as he ordered his men to abduct women or murder people who got in his way. Robert oversaw operations from his office on the hotel's top floor. His prostitution business occupied the eighth and ninth floors. From the seventh floor down the Damien was a respectable hotel.

Some of the women in his prostitution ring came from China. Others had been abducted in Oregon—lost, maladjusted, lonely young girls testing their hormones or escaping adversity. Most came from drug-addicted parents. Others had heard of the exciting lives that prostitutes led. It was often a step up from their own life styles, full of rejection, abuse, failure, institutionalization and rape. In most instances the girls were penniless and homeless, making them easy prey for Robert's pimps.

Robert first had the girls brought to his hotel for food and refreshments. If they had a drug addiction, drugs were furnished for them. They were treated with respect, perhaps for the first time in their lives. They were given protection, food, shelter, and clothes. Everything was okay until the girls found out that they would have to repay the kindnesses that had been offered them. After a month they were inducted into their roles as ladies of the night—either as streetwalkers, call girls, in local bars, at massage parlors or as night club dancers. Some of the girls found themselves rented out like furniture to wealthy young men with perverse interests.

As it turned out the racket was a prison worse then hell. If the girls escaped they were tracked down, beaten and brought back. There was no escape. After years of slavery Robert's prostitutes lost their luster. He tried to sell them to other local pimps. If that didn't work he drugged them and drowned them in the Willamette River.

One of Robert's other businesses was distributing pornographic magazines to local magazine stores. Another was loaning out money at exorbitant interest rates. If the money was not repaid promptly he sent out Sam and Denton. Retribution was swift, and usually fatal. Sam and Denton had developed methods of killing that looked like accidents.

To top off his devilry, Robert even rented out his wife. "Money is money," he mumbled. "I am better than any of the street pimps at managing my women."

Robert's wealth kept growing. Bankers loved him. Police were kept on his payroll. Outwardly he appeared to be an honest, respectable businessman. He dressed in new, flashy suits, and his shoes were so glossy he could see his own image in them. To him, women were nothing more then stepping-stones on his way to power and wealth.

Robert was smoking, ignoring his men across the desk, when his phone rang.

"Yes, who is it?" Robert said. "I see, and how many women do you have? Two? OK, that's fine." A smile eased across his lips as he dropped some ashes on the desk. "I'll send a man down to pick them up this week. Yes, yes he'll bring the money with him." Robert hung up the phone.

"Two more Chinese girls to add to our harem," Robert said. "The Coos Bay connection just paid off again."

Sam and Denton smiled. "Can we pick them up, boss?"

"Not now, we have other business first." His voice rose. "No screw-ups this time, understand? I've been informed that Charley Norman is taking a vacation."

"How did you find that out?" asked Denton.

"None of your business. I have my sources."

"Okay. Sorry, boss."

"Charley leaves tomorrow morning for the Oregon coast." Robert's voice returned to normal. "He's out to destroy us, boys. His most important source of information is my son's schoolteacher, April. He'll try to protect her at all costs. They must be together. Once she implicates us and Charley writes his column we're through. So make it look like an accident. There's no time to lose. Your reward will be the two Asian girls waiting to be picked up in Coos Bay.

"I'm thinking Charley will start his coast trip in Astoria." Robert snubbed out his cigarette. "It only seems reasonable that if he is going to look for coast stories, Astoria is the place to start before driving down the coast. He drives a red Chevrolet convertible, you can't miss it."

Chapter Four

"I'm afraid to go back to my apartment." April pushed the sun visor back in place and cranked the window down.

Charley carefully put Taylor's card in his wallet. He didn't want to lose it. "I'm scared too. My editor wanted me to get out of town because of the death threats. 'Let things cool down,' he told me. I thought he was right, so I agreed to leave tomorrow morning."

"Really," April said. "I'm worried enough that I'm thinking of going to stay with my parents in Brookings for a while."

"Say, why not let me drive you to your folks' home? I'm supposed to investigate the Highway 101 construction project near there."

April bit her lip. "I don't know."

"I'm not like Taylor. I'm a journalist. If you want a lift, I'll have room."

"The sooner I get home the better." April said.

"It might take us a few days to get down there. I'm suppose to be writing articles about the coast, but my expense account is for just one person. You'd have to pay for your own separate motel room."

"Of course." She paused. "Are you familiar with the road?"

"I've driven the coast many times. We'll need to start at Astoria. If we leave for Astoria now we can spend the night there. Then head for Brookings early tomorrow morning."

April looked up at cars streaming over the St. John's Bridge. She considered the newspaperman's offer. Her parents were probably worried sick because they hadn't heard from her. She had to make a decision quickly. She had clothes in Brookings, and she could buy others along the way. It seemed safer than returning to her apartment where Taylor's men would be expecting her. "All right," she said slowly, "I guess it'll be okay."

"If we start right away those thugs will never figure out where we've gone."

Charley turned on the ignition and the V-8 engine roared to life. He pulled out a dust rag from the glove compartment and cleaned the dash. Then he carefully wiped the outside rearview mirror. April noticed how fastidious Charley was. She didn't know if she liked that. He was quite proud of his car. It shined as if it had been recently waxed.

"Watch this," Charley said. Then he activated the convertible's top. It lifted off the window frame with a click and settled back accordion style behind the back seat. Sunlight flooded in.

"I bought this car six months ago," Charley said. "Its bright red color really attracts stares. This car has been, well, kinda, my obsession."

"I figured that." April took dark glasses out of her purse and put them on. Once back on the river road the wind blew April's hair. She felt like a movie star. The towns of Scappoose and St. Helens slipped by. At Rainier, Charley pulled into the parking lot of a small café.

"I need some coffee," he said. "Would you like some?"

"Could you get me a Coke?"

"Sure, be right back."

As Charley was getting out of his car, Sam and Denton drove by in a dark blue two-door Buick. Denton was at the wheel.

"Did you see that red Chevrolet?" Sam asked. "We just passed our pigeons. They stopped at that café back there."

"Pull over," Sam said. "When they leave we'll follow them."

"This may be a short trip," Denton said, his hair flopping. "It's almost too easy." Denton pulled into a warehouse parking lot and positioned their car behind some bushes. "Once we get rid of them, I got dibs on his car."

"You got it. I get the woman," Sam said. He pulled out his revolver, checking to make sure it was loaded. From another pocket he pulled out a silencer. He shoved it onto the gun's barrel. "I'm ready."

April watched as Charley carried coffee and Coke back to the car. He was handsome, in a rugged sort of way, she thought, but she didn't like his glasses or his obsession with his car. His bulky brown cardigan sweater and rumpled corduroy pants didn't fit the profile of a successful journalist. Still, she liked his red curly hair and blue eyes. He is brave too, tackling that big brute to save me. His editorials attacking the prostitution rings in Portland are simply courageous. But did she really want to risk getting involved? She just wanted to go home and forget about the whole mess.

Charley handed her the Coke over the driver's side door. Then he got into the car. Charley had parked facing the traffic. They watched the cars and trucks zip by while they drank. The sun was dropping in the west, 7:30 p.m. on a cloudless June day.

"We better get going," Charley said. Once again the motor purred to life. When they passed a big warehouse Charley noticed that a blue Buick pulled out behind them. On a whim he slowed down to see if it would pass him. It didn't, and he didn't like the look of the two men inside. "I think we're being followed."

April turned around. "Which car?" she asked.

"The blue one. Let me try something." He turned off on a side street, then reentered the highway. The blue car was gone. But a minute later he passed it, parked by the roadside. In the rearview mirror he could see the blue car pulling out behind them again. I'm going to cross the river at the Longview Bridge. We'll drive west along the north bank of the Columbia. At Meglar, we'll catch the ferry to Astoria. If that blue car is still behind us we'll know for sure."

~~~~

Back in the blue Buick, Sam was berating his partner. "Denton, you idiot. You missed the turnoff to the bridge. I can see them from here heading north. Turn around!"

"I think we lost them," Charley said.

"Good."

~~~~

By the time Charley and April reached the Meglar Ferry terminal it was 9 p.m. Charley purchased a ticket for the last crossing of the evening.

"This way," the uniformed sailor instructed. He waved them into a parking space on the boat's metal deck.

Charley activated the top to his car. The cover rose up over their heads and came down with a thunk as it locked in place. Charley hated parking so close to other cars. He knew some joker would open a door and dent his.

"Come on," April said. "Your car will be okay."

April led the way upstairs to the passenger lounge. From their seats by the window they could see a full moon reflecting in the dark river. A path of white light receded to the horizon, almost touching the moon.

"Finally I feel safe," April said.

Charley nodded. "I'm glad we weren't really being followed."

Chapter Five

Denton usually took orders from Sam. Sam generally had good ideas. Like Robert, Sam could get very angry if he didn't get his way. Denton didn't want to get Sam mad. He feared Sam's brutal side, more then Robert's.

Their blue Buick was the last one allowed on the ferry. Denton followed the sailor's directions and parked at the only spot left.

"What now?" Denton asked.

"There's not much we can do right now," Sam said. "Too many people around, and nowhere to escape." He rubbed his hand over his bald head. "We'll stay in the car and follow them when they leave. See their car over there?" He pointed to it.

"How could I miss it?" Denton said.

~~~~~

"I want to check my car, I'll be right back," Charley said.

"You worry too much about that car," April said. "And not enough about yourself."

Charley went down the stairs in the center of the boat to the automobile deck. He crouched by his car, checking it for scratches.

"That's him." Sam felt for his revolver. "If only we were ashore, this would be a snap. Bang, bang, and he would be out of our hair. Oh, oh. He's coming this way. Cover your face with a magazine." Sam clutched his revolver.

"Sam, I don't have a magazine."

"The car manual in the glove compartment, you idiot, quick." Sam covered his face with a newspaper. Denton pulled out the manual. Sam lifted his revolver as Charley neared.

"Not now, boss," Denton said, placing his hand on Sam's elbow. Sam lowered his head, pretending to sleep.

As Charley walked past the car he suddenly realized this was the blue car that had followed them on the highway. The two men inside had their faces hidden. One was reading, and one was dozing. Nothing unusual about that. Still he didn't like seeing the car again. He walked past to the rear of the boat. From the rail he looked down and watched as the water churned behind in a turbulent wake. The moon was sinking fast, half visible on the horizon. Another passenger joined him.

"The ferry will be going out of business soon," the man said. "They're building a bridge instead."

Charley studied the man, but didn't recognize him. "It's about time," Charley said. "They've talked about building a bridge for more than thirty years."

The stranger countered. "When it's built it will put a lot of people out of work. I'll miss the ferries."

Charley thought about all the people that would be put out of work when the bridge was finished. The ferry business was a tradition in Astoria. In a few years all that would change. A whole new culture of cars and highways would evolve, dissolving the old ferry tradition like a coastal fog.

Suddenly Charley remembered he had left April alone in the lounge. He nodded politely to the man, turned, and walked toward the central stairway that led back to the lounge. He felt relieved when he saw April dreamily looking out the window at a big commercial steamer that had just crossed the Columbia bar, headed upriver.

"Well, were there any dents or scratches?" April asked.

"Not a one." Charley sat down next to her. "But I noticed that same blue car down there with two men in it."

"Robert's men?"

"Seems pretty unlikely." He frowned. "Still, they covered their faces as I walked by."

April bit her lip. "What if it really is them, following us?"

Charlie shook his head. "I don't see how they could have figured out where we are. If I'd known they would follow, I wouldn't have asked you to come along."

April touched his hand. "I think we're in this together now."

Chapter Six

It was dark as they drove off the ferry into the city of Astoria. They hadn't gone far when they noticed a motel on Marine Drive.

"It's not the Hilton, but how about that place for the night?"

"It'll be fine," April, said.

"You know, I'm still worried about that blue car. I know they spotted my red car on the ferry, since it stands out like a Sherman tank. Let me try another trick to see if they're tailing us. I'll park over there in the shadows, across from the motel."

It wasn't long before they both saw the blue car, with two men inside, slowly drive south on Marine Drive. "My God! It's really them—the same guys who jumped us in Portland." "

"Murderous thugs," April said.

After the car had passed Charley decided to wait awhile. After thirty minutes he slowly pulled out onto the highway.

"If we parked at that motel they'd spot my car. Let's drive south for a while.

Soon they crossed the Young's Bay Bridge. A few minutes later they came to the Lewis and Clark Bridge. The roadway was tilted up to let a small sailboat out to sea. Charley braked behind a line of four cars.

"This will let Taylor's henchmen get further ahead. They might even turn around and come back this way. Keep an eye out for them."

At last the bridge tilted back into position with a loud thump. Charley started the car and slowly crossed the bridge, watching the sailboat's lights fade as it glided out to the Pacific. Charley drove on. When they reached the outskirts of Cannon Beach they still hadn't seen the blue Buick.

"I'm taking the old highway through town," Charley said. Taylor's men are probably staying on the main highway."

"I hope so." April had her doubts. It was still a long way to her parents' house in Brookings. She couldn't wait to get home.

They drove through the business district of Cannon Beach to the south side of town. Charley pulled over at a turnout that overlooked the ocean. White crested waves skimmed over silky sand.

"There's a path over there. Do you see it, Charley?"

"C'mon," Charley said. "Let's walk down to the beach." Charley locked the car and led April down the path. Half a mile ahead, Haystack Rock loomed above the waves.

As they stretched their legs, strolling the beach, April suggested "Why don't we go to the police? We should report these men."

"We could if we could find any police. They're scarce along the coast. I doubt they could do much anyway. It would be hard to make an arrest without probable cause. Those men haven't done anything yet."

"They attacked us in Portland."

"Without witnesses, it's our word against theirs."

"It's not fair," April said, pouting. "They can destroy young women's lives, and still go free."

"I agree," Charley said. "That's why I've been writing my editorials."

They walked along on the glistening hard sand, deep in thought as the tide receded. April brushed her dress down when a gust of wind pushed it upward. Soon they were at Haystack Rock. Then they turned around for the return trip.

Suddenly April stopped. "When you write your articles, you'll keep me anonymous won't you?"

"Absolutely."

~~~~~

"Checking out this road was a good idea, Sam," Denton said. He had parked behind some shrubbery across the street from Charley's car.

"I thought we should come back and check these turnoffs before going on. They must be walking on the beach."

Denton grinned. "All alone."

Sam's right hand went back and forth over his bald pate. "This time it really should be easy."

"What's your plan?" Denton asked.

"As soon as they're in the car we'll walk over there and surprise them. We'll simply bash their heads with our revolvers. While they're unconscious we'll turn on their motor, put the car in drive, and nudge it off the cliff. It will look like an accident."

"Pure genius," Denton said. "We'd better get out now, so we're ready to race across the street."

The two men crouched beside their car. Soon they saw the heads of their victims bobbing up the path to the parking area. Charley let April into the passenger seat and walked to the other side.

"Not yet," Sam whispered through the open windows of the Buick.

Charley opened his door.

"Get ready," Sam said.

When Charley closed his door, a car sped around the corner and turned into the parking space next to Charley, barely stopping in time. The young couple in the car began kissing and hugging.

"Hold off," Sam said. "Quick, get back into the car."

~~~~~

23

As Charley backed out of the lot, April saw the blue car behind them.

"There they are!" she cried.

Charley saw them too. "Let's get out of here."

April kept looking back. "They're following all right, but keeping their distance." The two cars raced through the tunnel at Arch Cape. Through Oswald West State Park, big old trees lined the coastal road. They passed over the Short Sand Creek Bridge, their headlights blazing off giant tree trunks in the thick forests on either side of the road. The two cars crossed the big curve of the Samuel Reed Bridge and sped around the steep face of Neahkahnie Mountain.

~~~~~

"Get closer, Denton!" Sam shouted.

Denton floored it, pushing the Buick faster and faster. As they neared the cliff Denton pulled up behind Charley's car. Waves crashed hundreds of feet below on the west side. A three-foot-tall rock wall edged the highway. Above them rose a sheer basalt cliff. Denton made his move and pulled over in the left lane alongside Charley's car. The two cars raced along at top speed with their headlights piercing the dark, like four motorcycles riding side by side.

When April saw the car zoom up on their left she screamed, "Charley, watch out!"

"Now!" Sam said. "Smash them into the wall!"

April's scream caused Charley to press hard on the brakes. They screeched to a halt. Instead of hitting Charley's car, the blue Buick roared into the stone wall, scraping and screeching along the rocks until it finally came to rest, smoking. The crash totaled the right front of the car and popped off its front tire. The wheel bounced along the highway a short distance, hit the wall and arced over the stone railing, whistling down the steep slope into the surf three hundred feet below.

Charley had been stunned by the unexpected attempt on his and

April's lives. He accelerated past the smoking wreck. He couldn't tell if they were alive and didn't want to stick around to find out. Had it been an accident he certainly would have stayed and notified emergency personnel. But these men were cold-blooded murderers. They might even shoot him if he attempted to help them. He made the decision to get as far away from the scene as he could, and heard no objections from April. His hands and feet were shaking.

"Are you okay?" Charley asked, trying to act calm.

"I guess," she said, still in shock.

"We'll drive to Tillamook and see if we can find somewhere to rest. We need to recover."

It was as if April was awakening from a hideous nightmare. She had a hard time pulling herself back to the present. "Sure. Let's just get away from here."

Chapter Seven

When the Buick hit the stone wall Sam's head smacked against the windshield. Blood splattered back. Denton was badly shaken but unharmed. The car was smoldering, with wisps of smoke drifting into the night air. Something sparked. Flames started licking out from the front hood.

"Sam, get out of the car!" Denton yelled. "She's going to explode!" Sam didn't move. Denton thought he must be dead. He quickly pulled Sam into the driver's seat, got out of the car, and ran for cover. Denton crouched behind the stone wall. The car burned like a huge October slash fire. Then it suddenly exploded, spewing pieces of the car and smoke skyward like a Fourth of July fireworks display.

Denton sat behind the wall, his back against the rocks. He tried to figure out what to do. He cursed Charley and April. He was still disoriented and confused. Everything had happened so fast. At last reason prevailed. "Call Robert," he mumbled. In the distance he could hear sirens. "I better get out of here," he whispered. Denton jumped over the railing and back onto the highway. He ran south towards the town of Manzanita. As the sirens got closer he hid in the forest uphill from the road. He watched as an ambulance raced by. Shortly, a police car followed. Denton jumped back on the road and scrambled south.

~~~~~

Charley and April heard the explosion, and Charley saw the fire ball in his rearview mirror.

"Tillamook is just 30 miles," Charley said. "Robert's men won't bother us anymore."

Still dazed, April nodded.

Denton ran along the highway until he came to a gas station on a corner. A street sign pointed west to the town of Manzanita. Denton exchanged a five-dollar bill for quarters. Then used the phone booth to call his boss. It was eleven o'clock. The phone rang and rang. No one answered. When Denton hung up he remembered that in order to reach Robert at night he had to use the code rings. First two rings, then three. The third time he had been ordered to let it ring until Robert answered.

"Hello? Who am I talking to?"

"Denton, boss."

"Are you alone?"

"Yes."

"Have you completed your assignment?"

"No." Denton explained what had happened and that Sam was dead. The car was a total wreck and he was at a gas station in Manzanita.

Robert sounded uncommonly calm and surprisingly unconcerned about Sam. "Listen, I'll get my car and drive to Manzanita. We'll get them. They might be overconfident now. That will be to our advantage. See what I mean, Denton?"

"Yes, boss." Denton felt somewhat relieved that Robert was coming.

"They may stop to rest, and that will allow us to catch up with them. I'm fed up with these two. Calm yourself down and I'll see you in about two hours." Robert hung up.

~~~~

After spending the night in a Tillamook motel Charley and April prepared themselves for the day. They were still wearing the same clothes they'd left Portland with. They bathed in their separate rooms. April had her make-up and combs in her purse, along with a small revolver. She was determined to buy some new clothes, especially now that they had escaped their pursuers and could breathe more easily. Charley, however, appeared in no rush to shop for clothes. April envied Charley and his red springy hair that seemed to be always combed.

They stopped at a downtown bakery to have coffee and a bite to eat. As they entered the small café they smelled fresh sweet cinnamon rolls, and the coffee percolating on a burner. They found a small table across from a case of freshly baked delicacies. A waitress with the nametag "Beverly" brought them a menu and offered coffee.

"Please," Charley said.

"Me too," April smiled, "with cream."

"I don't need a menu," Charley said. "I'll have a cinnamon roll."

"They're so large. Let's split one," April said.

"You heard the lady, Beverly."

Beverly brought the roll, heavily glazed, cut in half on two plates. Not far from their table sat three women. They all seemed to be talking at once. One lady laughed so loud it was hard for Charley to talk with April. The high-pitched laughter echoed in the small cafe. The noise grated on Charley's nerves. Another couple got up and left frowning as they walked past Charley and April, pointing their fingers at the ladies and rolling their eyes towards the disrupters. When they left they slammed the cafe door.

The discourteous group soon finished. As they left one lady was still laughing loudly. When the door closed it muffled her laughter and brought relief. April smiled and Charley let out a sigh. With quiet restored, Beverly came back to their table checking on their coffee. "You aren't from around here, are you?"

"I'm a newspaper reporter from the Oregonian. We're taking a trip down the coast in search of stories. Do you know of any?"

"As a matter of fact, our local paper has been reporting about a new type of balloon. It's housed at our city-owned blimp hangars. Tillamook recently bought the hangars from the Navy. A lumber mill is using one. The other is housing a secret type of balloon

28

being developed to fly coast to coast. Some crackpot balloonist claims his balloon will fly longer then ordinary hot air balloons. They've invited the media to look over their creation, and even take a ride. They want to publicize what they are doing. Their program takes place today at eleven."

"This is happening at the huge blimp hangars just south of town? " Charley asked.

"Yes,"

"Sounds interesting," Charley said.

When Beverly had left, April could almost see the inner workings of Charley's mind. She didn't like what she saw. "What about the thugs, and what about getting me home?"

"I think it will take a while for those bums to regroup, and this may be a good story. My gut tells me to look into it."

"My gut tells me I should get home, Charley."

"I know, I really know. But just give me two hours to understand this new type of balloon. Remember, I told you I need to find some stories to write about. I'll get you home, I promise. We have an hour before their presentation takes place. What do you say, April?"

"It does sound interesting, I guess."

"Good. Maybe we can take a ride in the balloon. I'd like to get some photographs and do an interview."

"Can I be your photographer? I've had some experience with 35 mm cameras."

"Sounds good."

They finished off the cinnamon roll and gulped down their coffee.

April understood why the balloonists intrigued Charley. The problem was that she had to notify her parents soon about what she was doing. She had to let them know she was with a journalist friend and it might take a few days before she would get home. She decided she would call them after the balloon event.

Twenty minutes later they turned east off Highway 101 onto a road that led to two massive hangars. April had never been this close to the hangars before. They were large, all right; they dwarfed everything around them. Charley had told her on the way that they had been built to house lighter-than-air blimps during World War ll. Big helium blimps were used to keep watch on Oregon's coast, looking for Japanese submarines. He had told her that the construction of the hangars required 1,700 men. When they were built they were the largest wooden structures in the world.

A crowd of several hundred people was forming at one end of the hangar. A makeshift platform had been assembled with a podium. Three men were huddled at the steps leading up to the rostrum. April couldn't get over the sheer size of the building. She could now see inside. It was the largest man-made cavern she had ever seen. Charley had told her about a plane that had flown through it just a few years earlier. At first she had scoffed at the story, but she believed it now. At the far end men were bringing out a big balloon. The balloon loomed over the crowd. It was attached by cords to a basket, big enough for several people. In the center of the basket were propane burners. The men secured the craft to the ground with thick ropes.

"Ladies and gentlemen, thank you for coming today," the presenter said. "This project has been under wraps for the last year. It had been a secret Navy experiment, a new type of balloon that can sail across continents. The Navy recently cancelled the program and told us our services weren't needed anymore.

"Now we are a private business, developing balloons for racing and long distance flying. We think this blimp has the capacity to sail from Tillamook to the Atlantic coast. The advantage of our balloon is its nonflammable helium, in the upper balloon. To increase altitude, we turn on our propane burners to heat the helium. If we go too high we can release helium from an upper valve. We've had numerous test runs so we feel it's safe for passengers. It is our purpose here today to attract interest in our project. Quite simply we need investors. We're hoping that there might be a journalist in the audience that we could invite for a ride?"

"Right here," Charley said, waving his hand. He handed his 35mm camera to April. "Here's your opportunity, April. What do you say?"

"I wouldn't miss it for anything," April said.

Charley took her hand and together they pushed their way through the crowd to the stage. "I'm a reporter from the *Oregonian* and this is April, my photographer."

~~~~~

Meanwhile, Denton and Robert Taylor were driving south on Highway 101. Denton noticed signs pointing east to the large hangars advertising the balloon's flight. He saw the large crowd of people.

"Boss," Denton said to his sleeping companion. "Wake up, boss." Denton reached his hand over and shook Robert's shoulder.

"What is it, you fool?" Robert opened his eyes groggily.

"We just passed something."

"What?"

"A crowd of people at Tillamook's huge hangars. A sign said something about a test balloon flight."

"Turn this boat around. Let's investigate." Robert lit up a cigarette. "Something like that is like honey to a bear for Charley Norman. Put the top up. We don't want Charley or that girl to see us."

"Sure, boss, anything you say." Denton activated the closing button on the white 1961 Lincoln convertible. He slowed and made a sweeping U-turn. They arrived just as Charley and April were being helped into the passenger basket. "Boss, that's them getting into the balloon basket."

"Where is Charley's car parked?" Robert asked, snuffing out his cigarette in the car ashtray.

"It's the bright red Chevrolet over there. I'm sure of it."

31

"Do you have a knife?" Robert lit up another cigarette and inhaled.

"Sure do."

"Do you know where the rear brake lines are?"

"I gotcha now. You want me to cut them."

"Puncture them, cut them, whatever it takes so the brake fluid leaks out. No one will see you; all the people are looking at the balloon. Get going." Robert knocked ashes into the ashtray.

He watched as Denton crawled underneath Charley's car. When Denton emerged he wiped his hands on his pants, folded his big knife blade back in the knife handle, and hustled back to Robert's car.

"Drive back to the highway. We'll hide somewhere off the road and wait for them to pass. Then we'll follow and see if you did a good job." Robert flicked his cigarette into the parking lot.

"Right, boss."

~~~~

On their way back to the car Charley and April were all aglow with their balloon experience. "I got some wonderful pictures, Charley. It was an incredible ride. I can't wait to tell my parents about it. Can I have some of the prints when you get them back? I could even show them in my classroom next year."

"Sure. Yes, that was very exciting. Thank you for helping me. Those guys really know what they're doing. When we get to the car I'm going to write up my notes while they're still fresh in my head. Names, the balloon's description, and what they're looking for in investors. My article might help them."

While Charley worked on his notes, April read the investor brochures.

When Charley had finished April said, "I need to call my parents."

"We can do it in Hebo, the next town. It's only about thirty minutes from here. I need to call my editor too."

32

"That was so much fun," April said. "Who knows what other stories might pop up between here and Brookings? May I be your photographer again?"

"You bet."

"I'm not pushing you too hard, am I?" April asked.

Charley looked up from reviewing his writings and smiled at April. "No."

"Do what you have to do," April said. "Don't let me rush you. I'll advise my parents that it may take a few days to get home. You need a break from your demanding editorials. I can see that now." April reached for Charley's hand. "I don't know about those thugs, but I'll take my chances as long as I'm with you."

"Thanks," Charley said, looking into April's blue eyes. "I don't want anything too happen to you, April."

She moved closer, and looked up at Charley. He couldn't help leaning down and kissing her, which led to another kiss. When their lips parted, April looked down.

"I don't want you hurt, either," April said softly.

"I just didn't know how dangerous it would be." Charley said.

April looked up, "It's not your fault, Charley." She kissed him on the cheek, and looked down again. "Robert has to be stopped."

"April, Your attitude in the face of all this turmoil is so admirable." Then Charley kissed April again. Their lips parted.

"On that balloon," April said, "you were like a child. You were so carefree, and so much fun. I had the time of my life, like nothing I have ever experienced. I'm now a photographer for the Oregonian newspaper! Charley, that was the happiest time of my life."

"Mine too." Charley said. "I suppose we should get to Hebo so you can call your parents."

Charley started the car. He was able to drive slowly forward past the other parked cars without braking. The Chevrolet gathered momentum to ten, twenty and then forty miles per hour, heading

33

west toward Highway 101, kicking up dust behind. Charley looked over at April and she looked back. Charley was beginning to really like this schoolteacher. When he finally looked back at the road they were very near the highway. Charley noticed a big truck loaded with lumber rumbling north at a high speed. Charley pressed the brake pedal to slow for the stop sign. To his surprise, his foot went to the floorboard.

"Stop! Charley!"

"I can't! The brakes don't work. Cover your head, April!"

April doubled up in a ball with her hands and arms over her head. At the last moment Charley turned to the right, heading north instead of south. The lumber truck veered left, trying to miss Charley's car. Charley's car brushed the side of the turning truck. Brakes screeched. Together the two vehicles left the highway, knocking down fence posts and plowing several hundred feet into soggy farmland before stopping. The truck's trailer tipped over, dumping logs into the field. Steam hissed up from Charley's radiator.

"Are you okay, April?" Charley asked.

"I think so."

Charley shoved open his door and ran over to the truck driver's door. The truck's window was rolled down. "Are you okay?"

"You dumb son of bitch! Why did you pull out in front of me like that?"

The driver climbed down from the truck cab and slammed the door. You could almost see fumes of hatred circling his head. He wore suspenders over a red plaid shirt and stood tall in logger's boots. He grabbed Charley's shirt at his neck. The trucker's right fist was doubled up and cocked.

Charley put up his arms to repel the blows. "It wasn't my fault. My friend April will back me up, just ask her." The driver threw Charley to the ground like an oil rag. Then he walked to the other side of his truck where Charley's car was mired in the mud.

"Oh I get it now," the trucker said. "You two were messing around, weren't you?"

34

"No," April said. "When Charley pressed down on the brakes, the pedal went all the way to the floor board. There was nothing he could do!"

"Oh yeah? I'll see about that." The truck driver flopped on the ground on his back, and wiggled under the back end of Charley's car. When he came out he apologized. "Some bastard really wants you folks dead. Your brake lines have been cut."

Charley came over to the trucker and explained to him that he was an *Oregonian* reporter and that a Portland mafia organization was out to kill him. Police soon arrived. Charley explained what had happened again to the officer who made a detailed report. The police officer called into Tillamook for a tow truck. A half hour later a tow truck arrived. It hooked up Charley's battered car. Charley and April climbed into the cab of the tow truck. Charley watched out the back window at the wobbling car as it was towed back to Tillamook.

Crammed in the front seat of the tow truck, next to April, Charlie said, "My car is a wreck. It's covered with mud, dented all over, no brakes, the radiator hoses damaged, the paint scratched. This car has been my pride and joy. Now look at it."

"It's not that bad," said the tow truck driver. "I looked it over. With the flat tire replaced, a new window, radiator hoses replaced, tires aligned, and brakes fixed, it will run just like before. You'll be back on the road in no time."

"I love that car," Charley looked down at his hands. Clasped over them were April's. Her warm touch calmed him. He looked back up through the window." Well at least the logger won't be fired. The police report should satisfy his lumber company. The police will investigate but they won't find many clues. It's hard to pin a crime like this on someone without eyewitnesses." At 6th Street the tow truck driver pulled off Highway 101 into a large garage and repair shop.

Chapter Eight

Charley found out his car wouldn't be ready to drive again until mid-afternoon the following day. April had been wanting new clothes. Before going to the motel, they took some time to shop.

The motel wasn't much, a typical Highway 101 single-story, with a simple gable roof. The owners lived at the short end of the "L," the part that jutted out towards the street. April and Charley both blushed a little as they signed up as Mr. and Mrs. Norman, for a room with twin beds. April had insisted on separate beds, although she allowed the single room, which was less expensive than renting two rooms.

"They're onto us, April," Charley said, taking one of the two cushioned chairs by the curtained window.

"You think the motel owner knows we're not married?" April said as she took the other chair.

Charley sighed. "No, I meant the Portland gang. Taylor's men must have been the ones who cut the brake line."

They looked out the window at the traffic. Between them was a small table with a telephone. The room had a small bathroom at the back. Separating the beds was a nightstand. A drab dresser with two pulls missing stood against one wall. The other wall had a counter with a sink and a hot plate. Next to the counter was a small refrigerator.

"Taylor's men must have found my car while we were up in the balloon," Charley said. "It didn't take them long to recover from that crash on Neahkahnie Mountain. They must want us dead pretty bad. Now we'll have to be constantly on the alert. I'm going to call my editor. I've got to give him the story of the balloon facility, and update him about the attempts on our lives."

April nodded. "I'll call my parents when you're finished."

Charley picked up the phone and spoke into the black mouthpiece. "Bruce Zeler, please. This is Charley Norman."

"Charley," the gruff voice from Portland responded. "You're just the one I needed to talk to. Things are breaking loose here. Because of your editorials the police made a raid on one of the prostitution houses downtown. A lot of girls were rounded up. A few pimps were put in jail and the johns were cited. Two pornographic magazines stores were closed. The city council is trying to pass a city ordinance to keep this kind of smut from being offered for sale. Ted Sutter got the story for us. He did a good job. We're covering for you as best we can. You really stirred up a hornet's nest. But they haven't found the ringleaders yet."

"Where was the house that was raided?"

"A drab old motel close to the courthouse. Why?"

"I'm with the witness," Charley said. "She's pinpointed the man in charge of the prostitution rackets. As soon as we can confirm our suspicions we'll be able to close down all his rackets."

Then Charley described their near misses with death.

"I read about the fatal Neahkanie crash in the Astorian newspaper," Bruce said. "Was the guy who died the same one who tried to kill you?"

"There were two men trying to kill us. Evidently one got away and is still trying to get us. I'm positive it's the prostitution ringleader's men. If I can just nab the one that is still alive, he might be able to positively identify the man we suspect as the ringleader."

"I have a hunch there is more than one man after you. The mafia boss wants you two dead. I think he's sent another man. I'm thinking you should come back now, Charley. We can provide police protection for you and your witness. I know that solving this case means a lot to you. But you are not the police. Capturing thugs is not your business. You're a journalist, damn it."

"Bruce, had we stayed in Portland, I'm convinced that we'd be dead by now."

"Who is your witness?"

"I can't tell you her name. She wants my interview to remain confidential. I'm sure she's telling me the truth. I just need a little more time to get her to safety. I need to get her home to Brookings."

"I know how hard-headed your father was when he was determined to do something and you're just like him. Damn it, Charlie I don't want to lose you."

"Bruce, I can't think of another way to handle this. I just need a little more time. I need your commitment to continue."

"Done." Bruce responded without hesitation. "I'll continue to tell people you are on a confidential assignment. You're playing with dynamite, Charley. Be careful."

"Thanks, Bruce." Charley said. "Oh, and there is one other thing that is bothering me."

"What's that?" Bruce asked.

"How do these men know where I am? How did they know I'd be traveling on the coast this week? You might investigate from your end. Somebody knows every move we're making."

"I'll investigate that all right," Bruce said. "Maybe they bugged my office. If so, we'll find it and use it as evidence. In the meantime you be careful and keep in contact. If I don't hear from you by tomorrow night, I'm calling the police. Understand?"

"Yes sir, I'll keep you updated." Then Charley told Bruce the Tillamook balloon story. After that he said goodbye.

After hanging up Charlie told April that Bruce felt certain there may be more than one man after them. He pushed the phone over to April. "It's your turn."

Chapter Nine

As Denton drove slowly north, he noticed a tipped-over truck and some spilled logs in the field beside the highway. As they passed the wreck, Robert looked to see if Charley and April were still alive. "Damn it. There's Charley and that log truck driver talking." Then losing his temper, "God damn it! I want those two dead!"

"We'll have more opportunities, boss," Denton said.

"Yeah, but I was hoping to have them out of the way before we picked up the two girls in Coos Bay."

"There's a lot of highway between here and Coos Bay."

"Here comes the Tillamook tow truck," Robert said. "It'll be at least a day before Charley and that school teacher are on the road again. In the meantime let's drive to Hebo. I need to talk with Grover to check on my businesses. After that we can eat lunch and plan our next move."

"Right, boss."

Looking back, Robert saw the tow truck hooking up to Charley's car. A farmer was using a tractor to stack the logs.

~~~~

"Hello, Father," April said. "I'm so glad to hear your voice."

"Me too, sweetheart," said Grant Lewis. "Where are you?"

"I'm in Tillamook. I'm with Charley Norman, an Oregonian journalist. His car broke down and we'll be here for a day or so while it's being fixed. It will be a few days before I get home."

"Are you all right? Your mother and I have been worried about you. She's is out in the garden hoeing weeds."

April looked at Charley and smiled, saying, "Yes, I'm okay."

Charley held up two fingers in a V. April kicked his shin under the table.

"Ow."

"Mr. Norman is working on stories for his paper. I can't wait to tell you about the passenger balloon we rode in. Tell Mom hi and I'll see you both soon. Bye."

Hanging up the phone, April looked at Charley and said, "I'm hungry."

"Me too. I noticed a Safeway store about a block away. We can get some snacks for dinner, and cereal and milk for breakfast. How's that sound?"

"Like a plan," April smiled. Soon they set out in the direction of the store. They had to pass by the garage where Charley's car was being worked on. Charley cringed at the sound of hammers, afraid that they were demolishing his dream car.

"It'll be okay," April said, sliding her hand into Charley's.

Charley's despair suddenly lifted. He might be losing a car, but perhaps it wasn't such a bad trade off, considering what he might be gaining. He couldn't figure out why this little woman could make him feel so good.

They both pushed through the double doors of the Safeway store at the same time, as if they were walking into an old-time saloon.

"How about a loaf of French bread, some cheeses, deli meats, and something to drink?" April asked.

"I'm for it."

Charley tried to pull out a grocery cart. It had stuck with the one in front of it. He pulled and yanked. Then the cart suddenly came loose with a loud metal snap! It flew into Charley's stomach. Charley and the cart rolled out in the aisle, nearly crashing into April.

"Do you have anymore of those tricks in your repertoire?" April said, laughing.

"Oops, road kill for dinner anyone?" Charley said. An old man looked at them sternly. A young pregnant woman pushing a cart tried to keep from laughing as she walked by.

"I know!" Charley said, "We need some wine to go with our French bread, don't you think, madam?"

"You need to calm down first," April said, pointing a finger at Charley.

Sometimes he could be a little much, she thought, frowning. But she was having a good time. And she didn't know if it was his right cheek dimple, his red hair or his piercing blue eyes she liked the most. She certainly didn't like his dark-rimmed glasses.

"Yes, we need to calm our shattered nerves," Charley said, lowering his voice. "Will it be red or white?"

"White for me," April said.

When they got back to the hotel room they set their bags of food on the kitchenette counter. April put the milk in the fridge and laid out the meats and bread on the counter. Under the counter were plates, knives, and forks, and a corkscrew. While April prepared sandwiches, Charley opened the white wine and poured some into two coffee mugs. They sat together at a table by the window, eating sandwiches and drinking wine as as they watched cars whiz by.

"I really don't know very much about you," April mused. "Oh, I know you're a crime fighter, and I know the story you told me about your mother and father being killed, but what happened after that?"

"I went to live with my grandparents in Eugene. Not much to tell, really." Charley took a drink of wine. "I went to Eugene High School. I worked on the school newspaper and played football. My football career was cut short when I broke my ankle. That's when I decided to concentrate on preparing myself to become a journalist, like my father. My goal was to write for the *Oregonian*."

41

Charley put his wine cup down. "I guess you know my father was doing the same thing, trying to combat crime and prostitution, when he was killed. He was trying to do something worthwhile for the community. But the racketeers had the money to pay off the cops and hush things up. There wasn't much I could do, still a child. That always burned inside of me. I want to continue my father's work. You understand, don't you, April?"

April nodded. "It gives me goose bumps that you care so much."

"After my father died I vowed that I'd enroll in the journalism school at the University of Oregon. Not long after I graduated, the *Oregonian* hired me."

"What year did you graduate from the U of O?" April asked, sipping her wine.

"1959. Why?"

"I graduated in 1960," April said. "It seems we have more in common then we think. Funny we never met."

"We may well have passed each other in the student union, or even sat near one another in the library and never thought a thing about it. We were both so engaged in our majors we never met. I wish we had."

"I feel that way too," April said, staring out the window. "Had it not been for Robert Taylor we never would have met this time either. That, Charley was a stroke of luck for us and Taylor's biggest mistake."

Charley agreed. "Together, we can outwit him."

"I hope so."

Charley finished his sandwich. When April finished hers Charley moved the table out of the way. He poured more wine into their mugs. They held hands as traffic hummed by.

"Enough about me," Charley said. "Tell me about you."

"My passion is working with children," April said. "They're so vulnerable and receptive. I feel I'm making a difference in their lives. My parents were very supportive. They paid for my college. I guess I was shielded from people like Taylor because I came from a small community like Brookings." She felt her hand being squeezed.

"My other passion is photography. I would've brought my camera but we left Portland too fast. My favorite subjects are ocean waves and boats. My bedroom walls are covered with my work. I've won several photographic competitions at the Curry County Fair. I even won a Best of Show prize at the state fair."

"You may take all the photographs from here on." Charley smiled.

"I took several photographs of a ship floundering at sea and of its rescue, " April said. Those pictures were featured in the *Curry Coastal Pilot* newspaper.

"Afterward, I got a stern letter from the boat's captain. He scolded me for the pictures being published. I guess it diminished his reputation, made it harder for him to get a crew."

"Yeah, but it also showed the captain's incompetence. Outstanding work, April."

"My boyfriend was on that boat. He never talked to me again. It really devastated me. I thought we'd been so close. I think I upset my father because I moped around for months. My mother finally confided in me, 'You were lucky, dear, that your love for him didn't go any further then it did.'

"It wasn't long afterwards that I moved on to college. I continued my photography at the University of Oregon. I even exhibited photographs in the student union. But, once I got involved in my educational career, that took precedence over everything. I wanted a teaching degree. Photography is still my hobby, but my teaching comes first."

They sat there talking and sipping wine. Night was descending fast. They watched passing cars as headlights flipped on, and watched as trees, bushes and buildings dimmed. Soon, it was dark outside. April pulled the curtains shut.

April undressed in the bathroom. She returned in long pajamas she had bought at the clothes store. Charley was already in bed. April climbed into hers and switched off the light on the nightstand.

Charley noticed a beam of moonlight splay through the bathroom window like a ray of light in a forest widening from the canopy to the ground.

"It has been a very stressful two days," April said, pulling the blanket around her. "You have an upbeat and honest attitude. I just want you to know I really appreciate that."

"Sure, thanks. I feel the same about you," Charley waited, hoping that she would follow this lead.

"I'm glad," she said. And then simply, "Good night Charley." April rolled over and said no more.

Chapter Ten

In a room on the second floor of the old Hebo hotel, two men busily studied a map of Highway 101. "There doesn't seem to be a place where we can get them, boss," Denton said. "Too many cars will be on the road."

You idiot, Robert thought. *You have no imagination. Sam had ideas. You have nothing. In fact you're responsible for killing Sam. I suppose I will have to put up with you, though.*

Robert lit up. Smoke drifted to the open window. Down below, log trucks rumbled by on the highway.

Robert thought about the big timber companies, and about big businesses in general.

I'm no more disreputable then they are. They exploit people too, don't they? I'm carrying on a business that has been practiced for centuries. Other businesses exploit employees with low wages and long hours. In my business I use different methods to train my girls. It takes courage to do what I do. It's like tackling a 300-year-old Douglas fir with a springboard and crosscut saw. It's like the big banks, taking risks to lend people money. If people can't make the payments bankers have to have the courage to call in the loan. It's not easy making a profit but that's business.

Refocusing, Robert looked down at the map on the table. "The map doesn't reveal Highway 101's terrain. Tomorrow after breakfast we'll drive the highway and see if we can find a spot suitable for an accident or a place were we can shoot them. In the meantime I have to call Grover."

Robert crossed the room to the nightstand by the bed. Sitting on the bed he picked up the black phone and dialed a number. He dumped some ashes in the ash tray.

"Hello?"

"Hey Grover, you son of a bitch, how's business?"

"Bad news, boss," Grover said in an unusually high voice. "Because of that newspaperman's stories the police are getting bolder. They made a bust on our little motel operation. Some pimps have been jailed and the johns were cited."

"Damn it!" Robert said, exhaling. "You mean I leave town for one night and this happens? What about the girls?"

"The motel is closed while the police investigate. The girls spent the night in jail. They're so dependent on us that they're no threat. They know what'll happen to them if they squeal."

"Don't lose those girls. They're some of our youngest ones. Be careful, Grover. With Sam gone, you're my most trusted man."

"Right, boss. As long as the pimps keep their mouths shut we'll be okay. I'll put the girls in our residential facilities for now. How long will you be gone?"

"Denton and I have to take care of that nosy reporter and the teacher. After that we're going to pick up the two Asian girls in Coos Bay. So we'll be gone for a few more days."

"I'm hoping you'll let me break in those new ones."

"We'll see." Robert said, exhaling smoke. "Now, damn it, hold that place together. I'll call again tomorrow night."

"Right, boss, I'll be here at the hotel tomorrow night for your call," he said as he hung up the phone.

"Let's get some rest, Denton," Robert said, smashing out his cigarette in the glass ashtray.

The next morning Taylor and Denton drove south from Hebo. It wasn't long before they passed the small community of Neskowin. A few miles later they came to a sign pointing to Slab Creek Road.

46

"I know this road," Taylor said. "It's a part of the old curvy Roosevelt Highway from the 20s. The highway department replaced it with a new straighter road further west a few years ago. The old one may be a good area for an ambush."

"Yeah, but how will we lure them onto it, boss?"

~~~~~

Meanwhile Charley and April retrieved Charley's battered but still drivable car about one p.m. Charley couldn't help feel pangs of regret at how his beautiful car was being turned into a wreck.

"Any more dents and it won't be fit for scrap metal," Charley complained.

"Maybe we can use it as evidence against Robert Taylor," April said.

"If my car's demise can convict Robert Taylor, then it will be worth it." Charley tested the brakes. They were working fine.

Tillamook receded behind them, the Chevrolet cruising at 55mph. Charley could hear some new rattles. He had to keep the car from veering to the right. Not a lot was wrong but it was annoying.

~~~~~

Up ahead on Highway 101, Robert and Denton were hard at work. They had found an old discarded state highway detour sign and moved it to the Slab Creek Road turnoff just past Neskowin.

"We'll wait in the parking lot of the Neskowin Motel," Robert said. "When they pass we'll follow them to the turnoff. After they've made the turn we'll throw the sign off the road."

"What then, boss?" Denton asked.

Robert thought, *Jesus, Denton you're stupid! Do I have to spell out everything for you!*

Aloud he said, "The old highway takes more time to drive and comes out at Highway 18 near Otis. From there they'll have to drive west to get back onto Highway 101. My idea is, after we pitch the detour sign in the weeds, we'll drive the new straightened road to the other end of Slab Creek Road near Highway 18. Then

47

we'll be traveling north toward Charley's car on a secluded road. Nobody will be around. Put on your silencer. We'll give our friends a big surprise."

~~~~~

The sun was blazing overhead. Charley tried to activate the car roof, but nothing happened. All he heard were a few clicks. Damn it, he thought, another irritation. They flew by the towns of Hemlock, Beaver, Hebo and Cloverdale. The next town was Neskowin. Just past Neskowin Charley noticed the detour sign.

"That's strange," Charley said. "The new highway looks okay to me."

"Maybe they're doing road work around that bend up there," April said. "We'd better take the detour."

Charley turned off the highway. They drove on the narrow, curvy road from the 1920s, under trees two hundred years old. Tall ferns crowded the steep western embankments, interspersed with the greens of salal and salmonberry. White cow parsnip blooms shot up at the road's edge between patches of foxglove and oxalis. Giant Sitka spruce trees, red cedars and Douglas firs clung to the slopes. Pungent aromas from the forest floor wafted in the car windows.

When they rounded a curve, April caught Charley's arm. "Stop the car! Look!"

Ahead a deer was standing in the middle of the road, looking at them with wide eyes.

"Why is it just standing there like that?" Charley asked.

April pointed to two spotted fawns stumbling out of the forest on wobbly legs. "She's protecting her twins. They must have been born within the last day or two."

The white spotted fawns tottered across the road and into the entrance of a small deserted campground.

"They're so cute!" April whispered. "Let's follow them and try to get a picture with your camera."

"Sure, why not?" Charley turned into the old campground,

barely able to squeeze his car through the underbrush—and hid the car in a campsite. They got out quietly. The doe had taken her fawns to a creek bank beneath a mossy big leaf maple. The fawns were competing to nurse.

April hugged Charley, enraptured. Charley gave his camera to April who managed two or three shots. When she looked up at Charley, she was smiling. He daringly leaned down and kissed her. They were so distracted while kissing, they didn't notice the swoosh of an unseen car passing on the old highway.

When the deer family moved on into the woods across the creek, April said, "I'm hungry."

"You mean?"

She batted his arm. "Not that kind of hungry. We skipped breakfast, remember? Let's find someplace to eat."

"Good idea. I know of a place in Otis."

They got in the car and pulled out on the old highway. Charley thought it strange that there was no other traffic, especially if this was a detour route.

April studied the map in her lap. "We should reach Highway 18 soon."

When they neared the intersection Charley pointed to the red neon sign advertising the Otis Cafe.

"That's the place. I want a big cheeseburger with greasy fries and lots of ketchup." They eased into the parking lot. Once inside the cafe they ordered their meals. Charley asked the waitress, "What's wrong with Highway 101? How come there's a detour sign just past Neskowin?"

"Nothing that I know of. I just drove Highway 101 myself on my way to work. There wasn't any road work. The Salmon River Bridge was okay too."

Charley looked at April and his eyebrows shot up. Hers did too. "You think we were set up?"

"They're out there somewhere," April said. "They must have driven past us while we were at that old forest camp."

Charley motioned to the waitress. "We'll take those orders 'to go' please." Then looking at April he said, "We better move."

~~~~~

"Where are they?" growled Robert. "Maybe they turned off on a side road. Denton, drive back through slow. Let's check all the turnoffs."

"Okay, boss."

"After they had driven a while Robert said, "There! See that gravel road? Turn off there and follow it for a while." Denton did as ordered. After they had gone a mile Robert ordered Denton to turn around. There wasn't much room to turn the large car around on the narrow logging road. The back wheels slipped off the gravel and into mud. The more Denton pushed on the throttle the deeper the tires sank. They got out of the car to have a look at the wheels.

The tires were almost covered in the deep mud. "Damn," Robert cursed.

"We'll have to walk back to the highway, and hitchhike into Lincoln City, Denton said. We need to find a service station with a tow truck."

"You thumb a ride to Lincoln City and find a tow truck," Robert said. "I'll wait here." Robert's facial expression hardened. "Charley and April will pay for this little delay."

~~~~~

When Charley and April drove on south through Lincoln City, puffy white clouds hung above the beach. The sun peeked through cloud openings, sending rays of light that glistened off the waves. To April it was quite exciting. They skirted Siletz Bay. Soon they were on the northern edge of Depoe Bay.

"This is the home of the world's smallest harbor." Charley said.

"I know that," April said. "I've lived on the coast a while, you

50

know."

"Oh, sorry. Did you know big gray whales swim in the ocean here all year?"

"Really? I thought they just passed through."

"No, here they hang around. We may see some today."

They were driving slowly through town with the commercial shops on their left and ocean on their right. April said, "Look, Charley! All those people on the bayfront are pointing to the ocean. Might be a gray whale like you said."

"I wonder." Charley pulled the car into a parking space. They got out and walked over to the crowd. On the way a big wave exploded against the rocks and nearly doused them with spray.

"It's a whale," a little boy shouted, dodging spray. "Mommy, Daddy, it's a whale!"

A man with a state park uniform and badge told an attentive group, "It's a gray whale. This one is on its migration north to Alaska where it will feed in the summer."

The little boy said, "The whale is looking at us."

The man with the uniform was handing out binoculars. Once in a while April could see the whale's back. He made a dive and his heart-shaped fluke splashed. The man with the uniform told those nearby to be ready. "The whale might breach."

April took a pair of binoculars. Just as she put the binoculars to her eyes the animal leapt halfway out of the water. "My God," she breathed. The whale landed with a terrific splash. Then it deliberately swam towards the onlookers.

April gave the binoculars to Charley.

When he looked through them, he saw the whale's eye, looking at the crowd. The whale was close enough that Charley could see barnacles and white splotches on the animal's skin. Then the whale suddenly turned and joined up with a pod of other whales. The group swam out to sea. "Thar' she blows," Charley said. The retreating mammoths sent spouts of white water up in the air. Within a short time the spouts disappeared altogether. The unexpected show was over.

April and Charley got back into the battered Chevrolet. They still had their lunches from the Otis Cafe. They sat in their car eating their lunches. Charley had to turn on the windshield wipers when the spouting horn sent spray up from the rocks.

Once they had finished eating April gathered their sacks and put them in the trash can. She got back in the car. Charley started it, and it purred like a well-loved kitten. "At least the engine is still beautiful," he said.

April tried to roll down her window. It got stuck halfway down. It wouldn't even roll back up. Charley looked the other way, frowning. He backed the car out on Highway 101.

"Be on the lookout," Charley said. "We know Robert's men are out there, but we don't know what they're driving, or how many men they have. I'm not even sure whether they're ahead of us or behind."

"That's the scariest part, not knowing," April said.

~~~~

Denton returned to the gravel road an hour and a half later in the cab of a tow truck. The big truck was covered with mud. Driving the vehicle was a stocky, muscular woman. Denton got out and joined Robert on the side of the road. The tow truck driver positioned the truck so it could pull the Lincoln out of the mud and then got out to connect the tow hook. She was wearing blue jeans, a dirty red cotton man's shirt, and heavy black boots. She hooked up the two rigs with the ease of a man twice her size. In no time at all the Lincoln was pulled from the mud and was on the gravel road ready to drive.

How much do I owe you?" Robert asked.

"Ninety dollars," she said, holding out the bill to Robert.

"That's too much," Robert said.

"Listen, mister," the woman said, "Those are the rates. Or would you rather me call the police on my radio? You can have it either way."

Behind the woman, Denton was taking out his revolver. He raised his eyebrow and tipped his head toward the tow truck driver, as if to ask Robert whether he should just shoot her.

Robert frowned. Murder was okay, but only if it paid. Dumping the body in the woods and hiding the big tow truck would be too much trouble, and too risky, to justify a ninety dollar savings. Reluctantly he pulled out his wallet and handed the woman a few bills.

The woman gave him a receipt and got in the truck. Before driving away she said, "A pleasure doing business, mister."

Denton and Robert got in the car. As Denton drove back to Highway 101 he muttered, "You should have let me off that broad."

Robert shook his head. "We've got to stay focused. Our main goal is to silence that newspaperman and his school teacher."

"We're north of Lincoln City. We could run into them anytime, boss," Denton said.

"If we do, we'll deal with it. There won't be any slip-ups next time, okay?"

"Sure thing, boss."

"That's better. We might as well head for Coos Bay and pick up the whores."

"They're not whores yet, boss."

"They soon will be."

"Okay," Denton said. His hair flopped as he jerked his head, watching traffic before making the turn onto Highway 101.

Robert knew he had the firepower to deal with his adversaries. Finding them was the problem. Highway 101 was 400 miles long. There were a lot of places for them to hide, but he and Denton would find them.

Then it would have to be quick, bam! bam!

Robert's hand smashed down on the dash. Denton flinched.

Chapter Eleven

Charley pulled over to the side of the road.

"What are you doing?" April asked.

"Going to see if this damned top will work." Once again Charley tried to activate the convertible top. This time it lifted off the front window but stopped with a screech, leaving a three-inch gap. He tried to reverse the procedure, but it was stuck in place. "Drat." He drove back out onto the highway with the wind blowing through. Charley had to reduce his speed to 45 mph.

"That sign says we're coming to Otter Rock," April said. The wind ruffled her wispy blond hair.

"The old highway loops through this community," Charley said. "Would you like to ride another section of the Roosevelt Highway again?"

"Well... okay."

They turned off the highway and drove over the Rocky Creek Bridge. From there it was like driving on the edge of the world. On one side of the road the land dropped off, making for marvelous west views through wind-blown spruces to the Pacific. The next sign had an arrow pointing west to the Devil's Punchbowl.

"Let's investigate," April said. "I've never seen the Devil's Punchbowl. What is it?"

"We'll soon find out." Charley turned right. A mile later they came to a headland that overlooked the ocean from a great height. Many people were there. "This must be it."

Seagulls flew overhead. Some of the people were throwing food for the gulls. Crows fought for food too. Charley and April walked towards the cliff's edge, scattering birds as they walked. Charley liked the salty air. Then they looked over the cliff. A stiff breeze greeted them. Sure enough, there was a big bowl carved in the sandstone 100 feet below. It must have been 300 feet across. At the base of the formation were two arching sandstone openings that let the sea enter and ebb out. Charley heard a man say the bowl was the result of a grotto's collapse. "That orange stuff is lichen," he said.

Also below were two teens, a boy and a girl, climbing on the rocks. Not far from them on another headland was a small colony of pelicans, and behind them some cormorants.

Charley noticed that the male teen was carrying a white sack, like a pillow case, bulging with something. The water had just ebbed out of the bowl. The young couple entered underneath with all the people looking down on them, as if in a natural amphitheater.

As the crowd watched from above, the young man put his hands over the woman's eyes, turned her around, and left her facing away from him. Then the young man looked up at the crowd and put his finger to his lips. He held up one hand as if to say: watch me. He emptied his sack on the sand. Then he positioned hundreds of sea shells into the shape of letters.

"Hurry up, people are looking at us," she said.

"I'm almost finished." The young man worked feverishly with the shells. Soon his cliffside audience let out a gasp. Faces smiled knowingly as the wind tugged at their hats and clothing.

He wrote, "Amelia, Will you marry me?" Then he got down on his knees. "Okay turn around," he said, loud enough so that the people above could hear him. She stood motionless for a few minutes, reading the sea shell message. She dropped to her knees. The answer was clear. They embraced and kissed.

As Charley and April looked over the edge she put her arm around Charley's waist. He casually dropped his arm over her shoulders. While the crowds attention was riveted below, Charley and April's lips came together too. They may never have separated had it not been for the jostling of the sightseers.

~~~~~

Robert was looking out the open car window as they sped along on Highway 101. Wind rushed past. He toyed with the wind by letting his hand fly up and down like a snake. *I'll need to be a snake to kill those two birds. They're going to ruin my business, and I can't let them.*

"Boss," Denton said. "Look up ahead."

Pulling onto Highway 101 in front of them was the battered red Chevrolet.

"Pull over," Robert directed. "Don't let them see us." Denton pulled over to the side of the road. "Let them get far enough ahead of us so we can just barely see their tail lights. Then we'll follow. It looks as if they are taking in the sights."

Looking at the road map, Robert saw that the next town was Newport. Also on the map was a picture of Yaquina Head Lighthouse. "If they're sightseeing they may turn off at the lighthouse."

~~~~~

Once back on Highway 101, April nuzzled next to Charley, her head on his shoulder.

"Charley, do you see the turn off to the Yaquina Lighthouse?"

"Yes,"

"I want to go there, too."

"Why not? We can't make it to Brookings today anyway. Maybe we should even stop at the Sea Lion Caves?"

"Sure." The couple turned off on the road to the lighthouse. The winding road dove and climbed through hills, ending at a loop with the lighthouse in full view at the edge of a cliff. White clouds floated behind the tall lighthouse. Seagulls flew about the tower like swirling snowflakes. A central vertical window looked out like the eye of a cyclops. There was a walkway at the top of the lighthouse, and above that a glass enclosure surrounding a huge array of glass prisms.

"We have to go up there," April said.

"If they'll let us." Charley parked the car. Hand and hand they strolled to the lighthouse.

A sign announced that the next tour was at four p.m. Charley checked his watch. It was 3:45. "We just have time to walk around the lighthouse." When they reached the back of the lighthouse they looked over the cliff's edge.

"Whew!" April said. A wave crashed on the rocks below, sending misty drops in her hair and face. When the spray had settled they observed a colony of black and white common murres standing on nearby rock outcroppings.

"What are those other birds' names?" Charlie asked. "The ones with the funny orange clam-like beaks?"

"Tufted puffins. We studied them in my classroom this year. They're beautiful."

"I don't know if I'd call them beautiful, maybe unique; certainly interesting." Further out to sea two fishing boats bobbed in the waves. Charley could see starfish clinging to the rocks below. The wind started gusting, bringing higher waves with more spray. "We better go to the tour."

Five people had already lined up for the tour. A mother with her two young daughters and a couple about Charley's age. "Mama, I can hardly wait," said the little girl.

"My name is Roger," the tour guide said. "It will be my pleasure to show you the inside of the Yaquina Head Lighthouse. But I must warn you, climbing the 114 steps to the top is not for people with weak hearts or bad respiratory systems. The cast iron spiral staircase is very steep. The tour will take less than an hour, depending on how many questions you ask. Let's get started."

Once inside the entrance Roger made sure the small group noticed the flooring. "Genuine marble."

"How tall is the tower?" one of the little girls asked.

"Ninety-three feet, the tallest lighthouse on Oregon's coast. It was first lit on August 20, 1873. The light still draws birds at night. Some of them hit the windows surrounding the Fresnel light. The first keepers used to eat the birds for food."

The small group moved over the marbled foyer to the staircase. Charley had brought his camera, and was photographing everything. He looked up the pole holding the cast-iron steps. "April, stand over there at the first step, I want to get your picture." April posed by the steps and stuck out her tongue. "Come on, April. Quit joking around, smile."

"Shall we begin?" Roger said. He started climbing the stairs. The mother and her daughters followed, the other couple, then Charley and April. Charley seemed absorbed with the geometric designs created by the staircase, taking photographs from different angles. He was sure to catch April with her many funny faces too. One of her poses looked like she was screaming with her torso draped over the rail.

Roger noticed the playfulness going on. About halfway up the stairs, he stopped and looked down at Charley and April. "I wouldn't make fun of this place. Have you heard about the ghost?" At the word ghost, April made a horrified face, which Charley captured immediately on film.

"Some people say the story isn't true, but others claim that when they were building this place in the 1870s, a strange death happened. The bricks for the shell of the building were transported from San Francisco. All 370,000 of them were unloaded from ships at Newport. From there they were brought by wagons over muddy roads to this building site. The outside walls are actually two brick towers, one inside the other. So the brick walls have a space in between. It was in that space that one of the workers fell. They were unable to get him out. Now his ghost shows up once in a while to harass unruly visitors."

April blushed. The group continued up the stairs until finally they reached the lantern room. Most were out of breath.

58

She watched as Charley busily photographed the hundreds of prisms.

"This eight-foot Fresnel lens was shipped here from France. It was designed to refract the light from a kerosene lamp out to sea, through concentric rings of glass prisms. Now we use a 1000-watt light bulb instead of kerosene. The beam can be seen 20 miles out to sea.

"The Fresnel lens was a life saver. Before this invention, ships were routinely lost at sea. They simply couldn't see where they were going. Augustin Fresnel's system of prisms was one of the greatest inventions of the 19th century. This is the original first-order Fresnel lens installed in the 1870s. The lighthouse acts as a museum commemorating and preserving this device. Well, that's about all for now. Let's begin the downward trek."

Charley and April trailed as the group began its descent.

~~~~

"Just as I thought," Robert said. "They turned off at the lighthouse." They slowly drove west over the long entry road. Coming up behind them was a Ford station wagon that wanted to pass. Denton pulled over. "I wonder what all the hurry is?" Robert and Denton took their time driving out to the headland. They turned off at a sign for Cobble Beach. There they found a beach covered with small rounded basalt rocks. Robert looked for Charley and April, but didn't see them. Then they drove to the turnaround by the lighthouse. There they could see the driver of the station wagon placing notices on car windows.

"Denton," Robert said, "get me one of those flyers. I want to see what it is all about." Denton stopped the car and got out. He chased down the man who was distributing the flyers.

"What are you doing?" Denton asked.

"The man could hardly hold back his enthusiasm. "It's one of the most remarkable things that's ever happened around here."

"Well, what is it?"

"They've finished the elevator at the Sea Lion Caves. The grand opening is today and tomorrow. One half price. Here take a copy. Don't miss it." The man got back in his station wagon and sped off.

Denton reported the information to Robert.

I wonder, thought Robert, *if the caves might be a good spot to get rid of our trouble makers. I wish Sam were around. He really had inventive ideas for killing people. He was an asset. Denton is a liability. I have to find a way to get rid of him before going back to Portland.*

"Let's drive to the Sea Lion Caves, it's not far. We'll case the site. That newspaper man won't be able to resist a news story like that. All we have to do is figure out a way to murder them there."

"Sounds good to me, boss."

~~~~

As the tour group was descending the lighthouse steps, April looked out the vertical window. "Charley, look!" Charley returned a step up to April's side. She pointed down at the parking lot. In the turnaround was a white Lincoln stopped behind Charlie's car. "Do you think it's Robert's men?"

"Could be," Charley said. "Let's get down there." By the time they reached the parking lot, however, the Lincoln had vanished. On their windshield was a flyer advertising the grand opening at the Sea Lion Caves, now with the new elevator. "That car we saw was just passing out fliers. We're a little paranoid. Listen, I have to see this elevator. I hope you understand. It'll be a great story."

Back on the highway they drove into the town of Newport. Presently they came to the Yaquina Bay bridge. Driving under the 600-foot arch April looked down at boats in the bay over 200 feet below. To the west, jetties pointed to the Pacific. Soon they were at the outskirts of Waldport. Greeting them was another one of Oregon's famous bridges. As they drove under concrete arches Charley was deep in thought already thinking ahead.

"This is going to be quite a story, about the Sea Lion Caves. I don't want to rush through it. Portland readers are going to be very interested in this new elevator."

"I'll never get home," April sighed. "Being chased by murderers, and cooped up with a journalist who is fascinated by everything. How'd I ever get involved in this mess?"

"It was your own doing, April."

"It was not! You bribed me with the offer of a free ride."

"If you really feel that way I know how to fix it."

"How?"

"I can put you on the coast bus, here in Waldport. The bus can take you home to Brookings. You'll be safe."

"Oh yes, you would like that, wouldn't you? I'm not leaving you to fend for yourself against these lunatics. And you know something else?"

"What?"

"I've never had such a frightening, thrilling good time in my entire life. What do you have to say to that Mr. Journalist?"

"I think we are both out of our minds."

"Okay," April said. "With that settled, what's your proposal in regards to the caves?"

"Yachats is just a few miles ahead of us. I propose we stop there for the night. The grand opening extends through tomorrow, so we won't miss anything. It will give me time to call my editor. When we get to the caves I can find the manager and write the story. What do you say?"

"I say let's do it."

"April?"

"What?"

"I'm having the time of my life too. Do you think, after this is all over, we could, um—-?"

April blushed. "Is that another proposal?"

Now it was Charley's turn to redden. "Maybe."

"First, let's survive these attempts on our lives," April said.

In Yachats they spotted a motel on the east side of the highway. It lacked ocean views and glitzy signs but promised cheap rooms. "Just what we need for tonight." Charley said. "Still want to save money with twin beds?"

"OK, as long as you behave."

Once they had checked in, Charley wasted little time and called his editor in Portland.

"Bruce, I have a great story possibility."

"I'm listening."

"It's about the Sea Lion Caves south of Yachats. The owners have just completed a three-year project installing an elevator. It replaces a steep trail and a staircase with135 steps on the north side of the caves."

"Sounds like a front-page feature," Bruce said. "When can you send it?"

"Tomorrow afternoon."

"Charley, I should tell you that another brothel was closed by the police today. They got a tip from one of the people caught in yesterday's raid. They still can't find out who is behind the whole operation. Be careful, Charley. The kingpin is still loose."

"I'll try," Charley said. "I'll call tomorrow about the caves," and he hung up.

~~~~

Robert and Denton passed by the Sea Lion Caves slowly. People were getting into their cars and driving away. Robert saw a man put up a closed sign.

"We'll find a motel in Florence for the night. Tomorrow we'll be the first ones here. We'll case the place and then set our trap." Robert looked at Denton. "Got it?"

"Sure, boss. Whatever you want. But right now I want a woman, and soon. I'm going nuts. How much longer will it be before we get the girls in Coos Bay?"

"Keep your mind on the road. You sound like a little kid. Where's the next potty stop, Daddy, waa, waa, waa. I'll worry about the whores, okay?"

After they had found a motel, Robert called Grover to get a feel on what was happening in Portland.

"More bad news, boss," Grover said. "This will be the last time you can call me here. I've been tipped off that the police will be raiding your hotel tomorrow. The police got a warrant to look into Denton's apartment. They found incriminating information against him and you. It didn't help that one of the prostitutes from the hotel was living in Denton's room."

Robert's face went red. He looked at Denton across the room. Denton was watching the TV.

Robert lit a cigarette. He put the cigarette in the ashtray. Smoke circled up. Robert felt for his revolver in his shoulder holster. Denton had always been a screw up, and now he was a genuine liability. But after thinking about it, he realized he didn't have a way to get rid of Denton's body.

Robert growled at him. "Turn down the TV, you imbecile, so I can hear what Grover is saying." Then he spoke into the phone again. "Take as many girls as you can to the hotel in Vancouver. Hide out there until I get back to town. If they close down the Damien, then we'll start working out of Vancouver."

"Okay, boss."

Robert put the phone back in its cradle. Then he picked up his cigarette. He inhaled, looking at Denton through narrowed eyes.

Denton's an idiot, he thought. *A sex-crazed idiot.*

Robert put his hand on his revolver again. Then he removed it from its holster. He pointed it at Denton. Denton happened to look at Robert.

"No, boss. Don't do it."

"Your sexual antics may result in the closing of my hotel. You had one of my girls living in your apartment. She ratted on us. You left incriminating evidence against me." Robert raised the pistol.

"Give me a second chance, boss. I'll make it up to you, really. I can explain. Please, boss. Gloria snuck into my room. I didn't give her permission to be there. She didn't get that information from me. She must have stolen it somewhere. I'll kill her when we get back."

"See that you do." As much as Robert wanted to pull the trigger, he still needed Denton. He needed Denton to help him get rid of Charley and April. He might need Denton to take the whores back to Portland. Robert lowered his gun in exasperation and placed it in the holster.

"Thank you, boss. You won't regret it."

The next morning Denton and Robert parked in front of the Sea Lion Caves building. The fog was lifting. The roar of the ocean came from below the cliff. They waited until the manager unlocked the front door. Robert wore his gray overcoat and a black fedora with a half-inch band. The brim was slightly turned down. Leisurely they entered the gift shop area and pretended to look around at greeting cards and other promotional items. Robert thought, I just hope we can pull this off without Denton screwing up. His carelessness has cost me my hotel. I'll get even with him before this trip is finished. I wish Sam were still around. We used to handle similar situations easily. Robert felt for the gun in his shoulder holster. More people were coming through the front door.

"Let's get a ticket and take the elevator down to the caves," Robert said. "Maybe there we can figure a way to do our work."

"Right, boss."

They purchased their tickets, then walked through double doors to a staircase. They walked down a flight and a half. At the bottom they passed through double doors outside. Before them the Pacific Ocean stretched to the horizon. Waves crested and crashed in thunderous roars on the rocks 300 feet below. Signs pointed to the new elevator. The wind was blowing so hard that Robert had to hold onto his hat. They walked down a switchbacking, fenced path. Behind Robert a man's hat blew off his head. It rolled down the steep cliff to the sea. Some women wore high heels. At the elevator Robert and Denton were among ten other guests getting in.

The first thing Robert noticed was the smell, a strong fishy odor that had been captured by the enclosed elevator from below. The elevator effortlessly zoomed downward 200 feet. When the elevator doors opened, Robert and Denton found themselves inside one of the largest grottos in the world. With the other people they walked down a ramp to a viewing area that overlooked the Steller sea lions.

Through a large cave opening below, waves pushed inward from the Pacific, washing over huge rocks around the cave mouth. The incoming waves brought more sea lions. They tried to crawl out onto the rocks before the next big wave. Big male sea lions had their territories staked out, and complained bitterly should another male enter it. The incoming crashing waves and the grunts from the sea lions made a deafening roar.

Robert watched the sea lions for a while. Denton's mouth hung open. Robert had to shake him, "C'mon, stupid." Robert pulled him by the arm to the back of the crowd. "Did you notice that small room over there?"

Denton nodded that he had.

"That's where the maintenance man works. I just saw him walk in there. Let's go." He led Denton to the little room, and opened the door. They both walked inside and closed the door behind them.

"What the—?" That was all the custodian was able to say before Robert's gun butt came smashing down on his skull. The man fell in a lump at Robert's feet.

"Nobody can hear us in here, Denton. The noise from the

ocean and the sea lions muffles everything. Get his keys and lock the door. Then tie the man's hands and gag him." Gawd, Robert thought, I have to tell this man everything. There was a peephole in the door. "We'll keep a watch," Robert whispered. "When Charley and April arrive I want you to devise a trick that will induce them to come in here."

"But how?" Denton said, his arms and palms out.

"They haven't seen you before. Just tell them you have something interesting to show them. Tell them it's in this room. An interesting fact about the Sea Lion Caves. Tell them they've got to see it. Once they're in here we'll kill them. We'll make it look like Charley killed himself after killing April and the custodian. A lover's quarrel? Heck, we'll leave it up to the newspaper men to explain it. Then we'll slip out of the building. For now we'll keep an eye on that peephole until they come in."

~~~~~

Charley woke up first. With the hum of traffic on Highway 101 outside, Charley thought about the latest developments. Robert's prostitution operations in Portland are being closed down. That is good. Yet his men are still a threat, trying to kill me and April. And, most important, Robert Taylor, their leader, has not been apprehended. Could April and I possibly help capture this notorious man? Things are coming to a head.

Sleeping soundlessly in the twin bed next to him was April. She is so precious, he thought. I must do the right things to keep her affection. I have to find a way to her heart. I'm getting close, and I don't want to ruin my chances. I love April.

When April woke, Charley had already prepared their breakfast of cold cereal, coffee and milk from the motel's supplies. When finished they set out toward the Sea Lion Caves.

Charley and April drove up to the front parking lot. A car was just leaving so they were able to park there.

"Do you see the white Lincoln?" April said.

"Actually, I do."

"That's the car I saw yesterday."

"It's empty," Charley said. "Let's take a look."

They walked over to the car and looked through the window. "Look," April said, "On the floor, a sheet of paper."

Charley tried the door. It was unlocked. He reached in and grabbed the paper. With April looking over his shoulder he read the words aloud. "Robert, meet Billy Winslow at the restaurant in the mezzanine of the Tioga Hotel in Coos Bay. He has your two ladies. Don't forget the five grand."

Charley and April looked at each other.

"This is Robert Taylor's car," Charley said. "He has joined the man who's after us." Charley wrote the contact information in his log book. He put the paper back on the floor and closed the door. "Let's go inside."

"I'm not going in there. Can't you see they probably have set a trap for us?"

"They can't do anything with all these people around, April. It will be okay. This is a big story. C'mon." He put his hand on April's arm in an attempt to lead her to the front door.

April, wasn't budging. "No." April pulled her arm away. "Do you value our relationship?"

"Yes I do, but—"

"No buts," April said sternly. "We have to leave right now. I won't take no for an answer. Somehow Robert got wind of your trip down the coast. We can't go in there. Do you understand?"

"Okay," Charley said. He hated to lose the story, but he didn't want to rile this determined lady—his star witness, and possibly his future fiancé. He had to admit she was right about Robert somehow knowing he was on the coast. They returned to the Chevrolet. Charley reluctantly started the engine. Then he backed out. Another car took his space immediately. Other cars were lining up. Charley pointed the car south. Then he said, "Next town, Florence."

67

"Can you see them yet?" Robert asked.

"No sign of them, boss," Denton said.

"If they don't show up soon, we'll have to leave," Robert said.

They waited another twenty minutes. The janitor's desk phone rang. Denton reached to answer it. "Don't answer that phone, you fool," Robert's instant reaction was to slash at Denton's arm with his revolver.

"Ow!" Denton pulled back his arm.

"We can't wait any longer," Robert said impatiently.

Robert looked out the peep hole. It appeared clear so he opened the door slowly. The roar of the cavern greeted them. He and Denton squeezed out. Robert locked the door. Then he forcefully slid the keys under the door. Then they went up the elevator. Robert was relieved with the fresh air outside. They got into the Lincoln, pulled out of their space, and headed to Florence.

"We better get to Coos Bay," Robert said.

"I can hardly wait to train one of the new recruits," Denton said.

"We'll treat them nicely at first," Robert said, "make them beholden to us. Then we'll start the intimidation. You know the ropes. Make them fear for their lives. After that you can be the first. Understand?"

"Sure, boss."

Chapter Twelve

Dark clouds pushed eastward above them. "Oh oh," April said. When the rain started, Charley turned on the wipers. Water poured in through the roof opening, and through April's window.

"I'm getting soaked," April said. "Find some cover."

At the north end of Florence Charley turned off the highway and sought cover under the Siuslaw River Bridge. They parked. Then they got out of the car and shook off like water-logged dogs. They got back in. April slid over on the bench seat next to Charley.

"You're soaked," Charley said. Charley wrapped his arm around her. They cuddled and smooched. Water squished from the seat to the floorboard. April ran her hand through Charley's soggy hair. They kissed again. Rain continued to smack the ground, puddling a few feet from the overhanging bridge.

"I have an idea," Charley said, sitting up. He looked down into April's blue eyes.

"Well, what is it?"

"When we get to Coos Bay we'll go to the Tioga Hotel restaurant. I'll say I'm one of Robert's men and ask for this Billy Winslow."

"What if this Billy Winslow knows Robert's men?"

"I'm going to take that chance," Charley said looking straight ahead.

"What about the five grand? We don't have that kind of money."

"I'll call Bruce and have him wire it to me at the First National Bank here in town."

"Charley? This plan is absurdly dangerous. It may not work, then what? I don't like it," April said, sliding away from him.

"Do I really have a choice, April? Robert killed my parents. How can I forget that? He threatened your life. Robert is committing murders. He's dealing in drugs. He's creating prostitutes out of young, defenseless girls. The note we found suggests that two more girls are waiting in Coos Bay. We both know that if Robert gets a hold of them their lives will be shattered."

"You're right, about the girls, but I worry about you. Maybe I could help."

"OK. How about if you take photographs of me meeting this Winslow man? We need to gather as much evidence as possible, don't we?"

"Yes. Still, we must be careful too. Robert will kill us if he gets the chance. I do have a small gun in my purse."

"Is it loaded?"

"Yes."

"Bring it with us. Come on." They got out of the car. "I saw a dime store up on the highway. There's a bank up there too. I'll call Bruce and have him wire me some money. While I'm doing that you go to the store and see if you can find something we can cover the car's roof with. Thick canvas, cardboard, anything just so we can cover that gap. Let's go."

"I'll look for an umbrella too," April said with a smile.

Charley found a telephone booth and called Bruce. After explaining what happened at the Sea Lion Caves he told Bruce about the money. "I'll need $5,000 to pay the gangster. Can you send it to me at the First National Bank here in Florence?"

"Geez, Charley, that's a hell of a lot of cash."

"Catching a big fish requires big bait, Bruce."

70

"All right I'll do it. I know your stake in this case. You have a young lady to look after, too. Oh, by the way, the police think the ringleader holes up in the Damien Hotel. They've got the hotel under surveillance. But they haven't arrested anyone yet."

"Bruce, I'm about to get additional evidence against the ring leader. I need that money to make it possible to convict him, and save two young girls. I'll phone you as soon as I have the proof we need."

While Charley waited for the money to arrive at the bank, April went to the dime store. When she came out she was carrying umbrellas, clothes, and some canvas fabric.

~~~~~

"Are you sure?" Denton said.

You imbecile, Robert thought.

"Of course I'm sure! That was April back there. Go around the block. I'll get out of the car about a half a block behind her. When you see me grab her, drive up to us and open the back door. Then get out of the car and help me get her inside."

April walked in the pouring rain. She was holding up a yellow umbrella with her purse strapped around her shoulder, and her arms were full of her purchases. She heard footsteps splashing behind her. When she turned to look, Robert grabbed her. Robert's hand smothered her scream. She dropped the bundles as Robert's other arm tightened around her throat. Robert looked around for Denton. "Where is he?" Robert mumbled. The Lincoln splashed through puddles and stopped at the curb, next to him.

"Cop car behind me, boss!" Denton yelled.

Robert took a glance back. He thought it was a cop car too. He loosened his hold and April stamped her heel on Robert's toes. Robert flinched long enough for her to break free. She splashed down the sidewalk, her purse slapping her side. She ran around the corner.

Robert looked back again. But it wasn't a cop car at all, it was a taxi cab. "Damn you, Denton," Robert said. "Wait here and don't move." With rain dripping off the brim of his hat, Robert ran down the sidewalk after April. When he rounded the corner she had vanished.

~~~~

Charley was just coming out of the bank when he saw Robert scrambling into his car. The white Lincoln screeched away from the curb, roaring past Charley. He watched as it crossed over the Siuslaw Bridge. Once across, it disappeared from sight in the heavy rain.

Charley ran to the dime store. Inside he found a shivering April hiding in an aisle. "Are you okay, honey?" Then he wrapped his arms around her. He kissed her forehead. She sobbed softly on his shoulder. Through the sobs she explained what had happened.

When she had regained her composure, Charley said, "It's becoming more important every minute that we have to stop Robert Taylor. Are you able to walk?"

"Yes."

"Let's go. We have to fix that car roof." They went outside and picked up the things April had dropped. Then they returned to the car and tried to mend the roof as best they could. "If our handiwork leaks we'll just open these umbrellas," an exasperated Charley said.

Fortunately the rain had stopped. They laid out some of the canvas on the damp seat. Then they squished down and closed their doors. April let out a sigh.

"It's not going to get any easier. Are you sure you still want to help me?"

"Even more so, now."

"Good. We're still a team. Next stop, the Tioga Hotel." Charley started the engine. Driving out from under the bridge they sought an access road to Highway 101. Once on the highway they stopped at a gas station.

Then they drove south.

Chapter Thirteen

Robert and Denton had driven past Honeyman State Park, south of Florence. The rain had stopped. "Take that turnoff to the dunes overlook," Robert said. Denton drove about a mile to a parking lot. Off to the west was a panoramic view of the Oregon Dunes and the ocean.

"We have to plan our next move," Robert said. He fumbled for his revolver.

Denton had screwed up so much lately. Maybe it's time. Still, Denton might be of use to me yet. That taxi really did resemble a police car.

~~~~~

Charley and April drove past Honeyman Park. "I wish we could park here for a while," Charley said, "It might relax you after that ordeal with Robert." April shivered a little, then moved over, cuddling next to Charley.

"You're my strength, Charley. Robert is such an evil man. You are the opposite of him, you have character. He doesn't know what the word means. I'm calm now, because you're here." She reached up and kissed Charley on his red stubble. "I love you, Charley."

Charley's eyebrows moved up, holding back emotion. Did she really mean that? Then April abruptly sat up.

"Charley, do you see him? That man over there? That's Robert."

"Yeah, I see him."

"Why is he walking out from the Dunes Overlook road? April asked. "Something happened back there. Robert would never be caught walking."

Charley kept driving on Highway 101 until it curved, out of sight of Robert. Then he pulled over and stopped. Charley and April walked back along the highway to see if they could see Robert. It started to rain again. They hid behind Oregon grape bushes and spruce trees. They saw Robert thumbing a ride north, back toward Florence. Then they heard loud music ripping out of a pickup truck. The truck passed them and screeched to a halt near Robert. Robert got in the truck. As the truck sped off, the only sounds left were the soft falling rain and an occasional car.

"Now's our chance to get ahead of Robert. We need to rescue those girls, and fast," Charley said.

Soon they passed through the town of Reedsport, then Winchester Bay, and then drove over the McCullough Bridge, a colossal series of arches and steel frames over a mile long," Then they passed through the city of North Bend.

Traffic became congested as they crossed into the town of Coos Bay. Looming up ahead was the tallest building on the Oregon coast, the Tioga Hotel.

"I've heard that the hotel is slipping into disrepair," Charley said. "A seedy manager has taken over its operation. Prostitutes work upstairs."

"How disgusting. How do you know all this stuff?" April asked.

"Rumors float around the newsroom. But it makes sense that Robert would pick up the two girls here. Probably trafficked from another country, then shipped to Coos Bay. I wonder where they are from?"

"Park in the lot behind the Tioga," April said.

"Can't," Charley said. "The parking lot is full. Anyway, its probably a better idea to park on a side street, someplace were we can hide the car. We'll have to walk."

74

Before they got out of the car, Charley took an envelope with the money from the glove box. He put the envelope in his front pocket of his corduroy pants. April made sure the gun was still in her purse.

~~~~~

To make matters worse for Denton, the gas gauge arrow rested on empty. Robert was mad as hell.

"You fool, you fool, you fool," Robert said. "Why didn't you fill up in Florence?" Denton tried the ignition switch again and again. Nothing happened.

"You stay with the car, Denton. I'll hitchhike into Florence and get some gas."

"Okay, boss."

Robert wanted to get away from Denton. He hated this idiot. His only recourse other then shooting Denton was to walk off his anger while getting the gas.

Robert walked the gravel road for a mile before he came out on Highway 101. Then he saw the red, crippled car pass by. He cursed silently. Then he crossed the road and put out his thumb. It had started to rain again.

He thought of Charley and that school teacher and how they were ruining his profitable business. It was falling apart in his absence. All because of Charley. *Charley, Charley, Charley, you fool, I will get you, damn you. You'll pay, and big time.*

Soon a pickup truck, with music blaring from open windows, screamed to a swerving halt on the side of the road. Robert saw a bearded man in the cab. His cowboy hat was pulled down, almost covering his eyes. The man was motioning him to come to the passenger side window. Robert approached the truck cautiously.

"Do you need a lift?" The truck driver turned down the music. Water dripped off of his beard and hat. There was a six pack of beer next to him on the seat.

"Yes, I need to get some gas."

"Well starch my shorts, get in. I'll take you to a service station. It's about two miles up the road."

When Robert opened the door he saw a revolver on the seat next to the beer, a rifle on the dashboard and beer cans scattered around. The man's breath smelled of alcohol. Robert climbed in, but he kept his hand on his revolver.

"Where's your car?" The man asked.

"At the end of the dunes turnoff road."

"Would you like to sell it?"

"Nope."

"What's your name?"

"Robert."

"What are you doing out here anyway?"

"Sightseeing."

"You liar. You're a city man. Why are you here? Are you a G-man?"

Robert laughed for the first time in five months.

"Listen bud," The driver said. "I asked you what are you doing in these parts. Now answer me." The big man slowed his truck, pulled over to the side of the road, and stopped. From his hidden hip he raised a hand-gun and pointed it at Robert.

"I'll walk," Robert said cooly.

"Don't move, mister."

"I'm from Portland. Just getting away for a few days to relax, driving down the coast. Can you think of a better place to go?"

"Come clean, mister. I'll put it to you gently. I'm running a business loaning money in Florence. I was just out on a debt gone sour, so had to kill this guy. I'm pumped. I also have a few girls that work for me, if you know what I mean. So if you don't give me some straight answers and quick, you'll be my next victim."

"I could use a man like you in my organization."

"You run a whorehouse in Portland?"

"Yep."

"Starch my shorts. Now we're talking. You're a badass just like me. I love it. My name is Jimmy." Jimmy put down his gun. He stretched out his right hand to shake Robert's. He obliged. "What a coincidence, two pimps."

"Sure," Robert said. "Now can I get some gas?"

"Yeah, you betcha."

They drove north to a gas station. Robert bought a gas can and filled it. Jimmy drove him back to his car.

"A Lincoln convertible! Nice car. Are you a crime boss or something?" Jimmy said.

"I have the biggest crime operation in Portland."

"Starch my shorts."

Taylor had had enough. He shot Jimmy twice in his beard. Then he got his gas can out of the truck bed and gave it to Denton.

"Put the gas in the tank while I take care of this corpse."

Then Robert went to the driver's side door and opened it. Reaching over the corpse he started the engine, and put the gear shift into drive. Then he pushed on the gas pedal, and jumped out. The truck jumped forward, gaining speed as it neared the cliff. It plunged to the bottom in a loud crash.

By that time Denton had poured the gas into the car's tank. He started the car and Robert hopped in.

Denton noticed the flat tire when he started backing up.

We'll never get to Coos Bay at this rate.

It took them an hour to replace the tire with the spare in the trunk. A few people came by wondering what had happened.

Robert told the onlookers, "A crazy guy just drove off the cliff. I'm going to report the incident to the police as soon as I get my tire changed. I have to go back to Florence anyway."

Finally Robert and Denton were able to drive back to the highway, but instead of heading for Florence, they turned south. Robert knew they had to get to Coos Bay, and soon. This trip was taking longer then he ever imagined.

Chapter Fourteen

Charley and April walked from the side street to the back entrance of the hotel. People were coming and going. A man with a sign on a piece of plywood stood by the door. The sign read, "Stop Wasting our Money!"

"What's going on?" Charley asked the man.

"It's a big informational meeting on President Kennedy's new space program. Coast legislators and reporters want to know what's happening. National space experts are here too. They claim it's a race with Russia to the moon. Not all of us agree and we're here to protest. We have protesters out front too. Why spend all this money to go to the moon? They're meeting in the big ballroom upstairs, in the mezzanine." Another man hurried past Charley and into the building.

Charley and April walked through the doors of the Tioga Hotel and into the central hallway. It felt like they had walked into a palace, with vaulted ceilings.

"You know, I've lived in Brookings most of my life," April said, "but I've never been inside this building." Supporting the vaulted ceiling were Doric columns, seventeen feet tall. Terra cotta embellishments adorned both top and bottom. The crowd climbed the central stairway, with concrete balusters topped with burnished wood rails. April and Charley followed.

From another spacious hallway they entered the main ballroom. The same Doric theme accented the cavernous room, but here the columns were eighteen feet tall. In the center of the vaulted room hung huge chandeliers. Big half-moon windows looked out on the streets. Chairs had been arranged for a hundred people, with a stage at the far end of the room. People filed along the tiled floor to their seats. The informational meeting was about to begin. A man at the podium knocked his knuckle on the microphone. It echoed as if in a cave.

"There's the entrance door to the lounge, through that partition," Charley said. "I want you to stay here in the main room. After about ten minutes come into the lounge and take a table across the room from me. We have to figure out how to move the girls out of the bar and into my car."

"Okay," April said.

From the brightly lit cavern, Charley entered the darkened lounge area. He had to wait at the door to let his eyes adjust. In the bar there was the clinking of glasses, and loud talking. People started leaving when they heard the moderator start the proceedings. That freed up a table by the wall. Charley quickly took it. Across from him was a long bar that stretched across the room. Several people remained on the bar stools. On the exterior walls the half round windows were covered with dingy draperies. Most of the reporters and dignitaries had already adjourned to the adjoining room. Charley could hear the muffled voice of the moderator.

A waitress with a short skirt and a blouse opened at the top, approached his table. She wore a name tag: Sarah.

"Drink, mister?"

"I'll have a bottle of Olympia."

"Be right back." Soon she returned with a glass and a bottle of cold beer dripping with condensed water. As she placed the items on the table Sarah bent over, displaying her cleavage. Her eyebrows lifted as she said, "Will there be anything else?"

Charley replied calmly, "Not right now, Sarah."

"One dollar, please."

Charley dug into his back pocket for his wallet. He produced the money, plus a one dollar tip.

"Thanks, mister,"

Charley nursed his beer for about five minutes. Then he motioned for Sarah.

"Yes?"

"Is Billy here?"

"Who's calling?"

"Charley, Robert Taylor's man. He'll understand."

"Okay." Sarah went over to the bartender and talked with him in a hushed voice.

The bartender was a short man, very stocky with broad shoulders and thick dark hair parted down the middle. He had a white towel over his shoulder. He came over and sat down at the table. "Did you bring the money?"

"Yes. Can I see the girls?"

"Let me see the money."

Charley produced a cashier's check for $5,000. "When you give me the girls, I'll give you the money, Okay?"

"Fair enough. You know I'd almost given up on you. I thought if you didn't come I'd keep the broads myself. You know, I could use them in my operation here. But a deal is a deal. Let me go get them." Billy stood up and left the room by a door behind the bar.

Charley stood up to stretch his legs. From the windows he saw some anti-government protesters on the front sidewalk below. He returned to his seat. Meanwhile April walked past him to sit at another table.

"I'll have a mai-tai," she told Sarah. She made casual eye contact with Charley. A man from the bar came over to her table.

"Can I join you?"

"No."

He sat down anyway.

"If you don't leave, I'll call for help. Leave me alone."

The man staggered back to his bar stool.

They waited for what seemed like ages, but could not really have been more than a quarter hour. Charley could hear the muted speakers in the next room. He noticed a man by the window who parted the curtains and kept looking down at the protesters. He too was sipping a beer.

Finally Billy appeared, leading two Chinese girls to Charley's table. One seemed about seventeen years old. The other looked about eleven. They wore mussed, flower-patterned dresses. Charley felt for the envelope in his pocket.

"They're sisters. They don't speak English," Billy said. "The older girl sitting next to me is called Su. Her sister's name is Ming. Will they work out for you?"

"Yes."

"Well, what about the money? No stalling."

Charley looked over at April and nodded. "I'm not stalling," Charley said. He pulled out the money and gave it to Billy.

April took the photograph and the bulb flashed.

"What's going on here?"

At the same time Sarah came to the table.

"Billy, there's an urgent call for you at the bar."

Billy got up. "I'll be right back, mister. Don't leave."

Charley reached into his pocket for another envelope. From the envelope he took out a piece of paper with symbols on it. One of the symbols was a swastika, the other was a bold red cross. He showed it to Sue and held his fingers in a cross. Then he pointed to himself. Then he pointed to the swastika, ran his hand across his throat, and pointed at Billy.

April wondered what he was doing. Then she saw the older sister smile and nod her head in understanding.

The man sipping a beer near the window signaled the protesters below with a hand wave. Then he lit his cigarette lighter and set fire to the window drapes. The flames shot upward, climbing the wall to the ceiling. He then shouted, "Fire!"

People ran from the lounge down the north stairs. Some ran through the partition doorway and into the big meeting room. Smoke billowed through that door like a dark storm cloud. The speaker tried to calm the crowd. But most people panicked, clogging the stairwell.

Charley led the girls out the north stairwell up to the second floor. April followed.

What is he doing? she thought.

Then he pushed the elevator button. When the doors opened they all got in. He pushed the ninth floor button.

"Are you crazy!" April said. "The building is on fire and we're going up?"

"I know what I'm doing. Tell you later."

The elevator reached the ninth floor and the doors opened. Charley led the way out, holding Su's hand. He took everyone to the window at the north end of the hall.

"April, get on my shoulders and pull down that trap door!" She did, and a folding ladder shot down to the hallway floor. They went up the ladder to the roof. Charley pulled the ladder up, closing the trap door. They were now on the roof, an area about one hundred feet square. A three-foot wall encircled the roof edge. Two decorative urns perched precariously on top of the wall.

"Don't look over the side," Charley warned. "People will be looking up. We don't want them to see us up here."

"What is going on?" April demanded.

"I thought this would be the safest place for us, April. You know when I told you about the rumors that circulated in the newsroom? Well when one reporter did a story on this building he told us that it was fireproof. The building is solid reinforced concrete. Each floor is concrete and the room partitions are made from tile. I knew that the fire couldn't spread, and felt that Billy might send his men after us. So I decided to head for the roof. No one would think to look up here. It's like being on top of a concrete parking lot. When everything is back to calm, we'll slip back down via the fire escape. Then we'll make a run for the car."

"But how come the girls came with us, so obediently?" April asked.

"I showed them pictures of a swastika and a red cross. Fortunately Su understood." Su smiled as Charley was talking. While we are up here let's try to get to know each other." They all sat down with their backs against the wall.

Through hand motions, and facial expressions, Charley and April were able to show the girls that they were safe. They also were able to convey that Billy was a bad man. When the explanations were made, the girls bowed their heads in smiles and appreciation.

Charley tried to convey that their troubles weren't over, that another bad man was after them, and he would stop at nothing until the girls were back in his possession. That he wanted Charley and April dead. This took a lot of imaginative hand signals to convey. Then they settled down to wait until nightfall.

~~~~

At Reedsport Robert decided he'd better call Billy. Robert knew that he was late, so he wanted to assure Billy that he and Denton would be there soon.

Sarah answered the phone. "I'll get Billy."

"This is Billy. What is it?"

"Billy, I'll be there in about an hour."

"What?" Billy said. "Didn't you send a man for the girls? That's what you told me you were going to do."

"I know, but things have changed," Robert said.

"Your man just paid me $5,000 for the girls."

"What man?"

"Charley."

"He's a journalist trying to bust our Portland rackets. Hold him, don't let him out of your sight."

"Hey, I think his friend just took a picture of me taking the money. Hey, wait! My lounge is on fire." Billy dropped the phone. He got a fire extinguisher from under the bar and rushed over to the drapes.

"Don't hang up, Billy! Billy?" Robert put the phone down and hurried back to his car.

A half hour later he and Denton drove over the McCullough bridge into North Bend. Next came Coos Bay. "Maybe that son of a bitch Charley is still here," Robert said.

"Let's drive around the hotel and see if we can spot them."

On a side street they noticed Charley's car. "Slow down Denton, stop right here." Robert got out of the car, pulled out his revolver, and shot two bullets into the Chevrolet's radiator. Water began dribbling out.

"He won't go far in that wreck." Robert quickly got back into the Lincoln.

He told Denton to drive to the front of the Tioga Hotel. The anti-government protesters had left. A firetruck was just leaving as they parked in front of the hotel. The fire had been extinguished. They took the north stairwell to the mezzanine lounge. The smell of burnt drapes and tables lingered. Sarah and Billy were cleaning up. Billy looked mad as hell.

"What's going on, Billy?" Robert said.

"That asshole, Charley, paid me for the girls, photographed it, and then left when the fire started. I didn't have time to stop him because of the fire. My men have looked all over for them. But they've disappeared."

"Charley stole my girls? Damn it, Billy, you botched it." Robert thought a moment. "I know they haven't left town yet, because their car is still parked behind the hotel. How long ago did they leave?"

"About an hour ago," Billy said. "Look, I'm sorry about what happened. But under the circumstances I didn't have much choice. That damned government protestor set fire to my place. The conference was giving me some good business. I needed that money to pay for last month's rent. I have two girls working upstairs plus Sarah here. Even so, business has been slow. Then that damed protestor, and the fire trucks.

"Fortunately I work in a concrete coffin, not much to burn. I'm afraid I just lost my concentration. That bastard Charley took advantage of me. I need to reopen as fast as possible. I need the five grand he gave me. Sorry, man. My men are still out there, trying to find them."

"I sabotaged their car, so they can't go too far," Robert said. "Oh yes, I want you to meet my associate, Denton."

They shook hands. "I have to make a call to my business manager, Grover, in Portland right away."

"I have an idea," Billy said. "Why don't you and Denton take a room for the night. The hotel has lots of empty rooms, some with great views. Why not spend the night here? The registration counter is downstairs in the lobby. When my men find Charley and the girls we'll have the clerk call you."

"To tell you the truth, I am tired. And I need to make that call. Tomorrow's a clean slate. I'll figure out what to do then. Call us right away if you find them. Your men know where to look better then we do."

"Good," Billy said. "Have Janice at the registration desk tell me which room you're in. I'll notify you immediately when we have them."

Robert and Denton left to check in at the registration desk. After they had settled in to their room, Robert picked up the phone and called Portland.

"Grover here."

"Any more news?"

"Boss, I feel as though something's up. Can't explain it. It's just too quiet."

"Wait till tomorrow, then pull out. Be sure to take my records from the lower left desk drawer. Leave everything else in place. Go to the Vancouver hotel and wait for me to call. You got it?"

"Sure, boss."

"Denton and I have some unfinished business here in Coos Bay. I'll call you at the Vancouver office in a few days."

"Wait, boss. One other thing might be important to you. Is that school teacher April still with Charley?"

"Yes, why?"

"Monica said that April was probably riding with Charley because her parents live in Brookings. Monica said she learned about April's parents in one of those student conference meetings."

"Interesting," Robert said. "Do you know their last name?"

"Monica thinks it's the same as their daughter's name, Lewis."

"Thanks, Grover. That explains why Charley and April are still together. Talk to you in a few days."

"Denton, I have a job for you. Tomorrow, I want you to take the bus to Brookings. Find out where April's parents live. Case their place and their habits. When I get to Brookings we'll meet on the Chetco Bridge between Brookings and the city of Harbor. Look here on the map. Do you see it?"

"Yes, boss."

"After you have that information stay close to the bridge.

If I haven't silenced Charley and April by then, we'll start working on April's parents. Maybe take them hostage. If we have them, we might be able to work out a trade. Their last name is Lewis. Should be listed in a Brookings phone book."

"Gotcha."

Robert and Denton were tired. They lay down on their beds and were soon snoring.

Billy Winslow and Sarah had worked feverishly to get the bar back in order for customers. Travis, the bouncer, was back on duty.

Billy's other men were still outside searching for Charley's group. They had been told to search nearby neighborhoods.

"Honey, I think we're ready to open back up," Sarah said. She liked being Billy's number one woman. The two other prostitutes were Chinese. Once in a while they tried to take Billy from her, but she always prevailed. Billy counted on her. They had a business going, and when there were conventions or meetings in the big ballroom, business was really good. Billy shared a few dollars with her when that happened. With the bar, the girls upstairs, and the money she brought in, she and Billy were putting a few bucks in the bank.

As long as the girls upstairs behaved, Billy wouldn't beat them. But when they didn't mind him or tried to escape, Billy would lose his temper. He had ways of catching them. Then, sometimes, he would beat them, or knock them unconscience, and they wouldn't be able to work for a few days with all the bruises.

When he's mad he scares me too, Sarah thought. I wish he wasn't so mean with them.

"It's ten p.m." Billy said. "Let's open up. Sarah, take the 'open' signs downstairs and put them on the sidewalk."

It didn't take long for a few locals to start trickling in, most of them local drunks. They aligned themselves on stools at the long bar. Billy poured the drinks.

~~~~

About 3 a.m. Charley realized it was now or never. He woke everyone up. Charley looked over the north railing. He saw street lights below. A pair of small headlights were driving south slowly past the Tioga. Charley reasoned the only safe way to access the fire escape was to go back down the trap door to the ninth floor hall, then climb through the north window. He put his finger to his lips. With hand motions and whispers he explained the method of descent.

Charley lowered the trap door. He was the first one down the ladder. Then he beckoned the rest to come down. When they were all in the hall, Charley closed the trap door. Charley led them to the window. They all climbed out onto the fire escape, and carefully descended from floor to floor. When they reached the fourth floor they all froze. Coming out the bar's exit door below them were drunken revelers. The bar had just closed. Travis was leading the throng outside. He heard creaking from the metal fire escape above him. He looked up and noticed the climbers.

"Hey Billy, come out here quick. That journalist and his friends are on the fire escape."

"You stay here, Travis, I'll go inside and wait at the elevator. They have to come down one of those ways. Have your gun out. Don't let them go anywhere." Billy ran though the lobby. On his way he told Janice to call Robert's room. "Tell him we've found Charley and the girls. Tell him to come to the ballroom right away."

"We've been spotted," April said.

"This way," Charley said. He led them through the fourth floor window and into the hallway. Then they ran down a flight of stairs to the second floor. From the second floor they found the central stairway that led down to the mezzanine ballroom. As they walked across the ballroom they heard Robert's voice.

"Hold it!"

The group froze.

Billy and Travis entered the room with their weapons drawn. Sarah peeked in from the lounge door. Charley and the girls huddled in the center of the ballroom under the huge chandelier. Billy grabbed Su and dragged her over to Robert.

"I believe Su is yours," Billy said.

Robert drew back his right arm and smacked Su so hard that it sent her sprawling across the room. "Handcuff her, Denton."

Sarah rushed into the room and put her arms around Ming. "Don't hurt Ming please, she's too young."

"Just a minute!" a voice roared from the stairway entrance. It was a barrel-chested man standing at least six feet four inches tall. In his hands was a sawed off shotgun. "Drop those guns, and get your hands up in the air." Guns crashed on the tile. "I'm Floyd Mason, the hotel owner. Billy, what's going on here? I heard about the fire and came as soon as I could."

"Well sir, this is what happened." Billy tried to explain.

"This is the way I see it, Billy." Floyd said. "You are running a small-time prostitution business in my hotel. You're also selling girls to other prostitution houses.

"According to Billy, the girls are Robert Taylor's property. Charley tried a squeeze play, lied to Billy and got the girls. That right, Billy?"

"Yes, sir."

"You have it right, Mr. Mason." Charley said. "I paid 5,000 bucks for these two ladies. April has the transaction on film. We were going to use this information to indict Robert Taylor for his prostitution houses in Portland. Hopefully we can close his businesses down."

"Shut up, Charley," Floyd said. "Billy, I want you to return the $5,000 to Charley."

Billy pulled the check from his pocket and gave it to Charley.

"Robert, it's now your turn. Pay Billy the $5,000 you promised."

"Gladly," Robert said. He produced the money from his wallet and gave it to Billy. Robert, take the handcuffs off Su."

Robert nodded to Denton, who removed the cuffs.

"Where are you parked, Robert?" Floyd said.

"Out front."

"I want you and Denton to go out to your car and wait until I bring the girls to you. I have some unfinished business with Billy, then I'll be right out." Robert bent down to pick up his revolver. Floyd stopped him. "Leave it."

Robert and Denton left for their car.

"Billy, you're lucky to be alive. You and your sleazy businesses have turned my hotel into a disreputable whorehouse. Sarah, I want you and your other girls to get out of my hotel. You can pay me whatever rent you owe me from Robert's money. Leave it in the lounge. I never want to see either of you around my hotel again. Get moving." When Billy and his men and Sarah had left, Floyd Mason turned his attention to Charley.

"Charley, you and your girlfriend can take Su and Ming. I don't plan on giving them to Robert." Su was struggling to her feet. Floyd continued, "I know who you are, Charley. You're that journalist working for the *Oregonian* trying to bust up the prostitution rings. Take these young girls to safety, and good luck to you."

Charley and April led the girls to the back exit. Once outside they hustled to Charley's battered car. It wasn't long before they were headed south on the coast highway.

~~~~~

Robert knew he had been set up. Floyd never showed up with the girls. Instead Billy left the hotel, and warned Robert to get out of town. Robert decided it would be safest to get away from Highway 101 for a while. He instructed Denton to drive north. When they reached the turnoff to Shore Acres and the Pacific Ocean he told Denton to take it. They ended up at the Shore Acres overlook. Denton parked the car. It was around 5 a.m. The clouds in the east were getting lighter. Denton fell asleep, his head slumped forward, snoring like a hive of bees. Robert got out of the car and walked to the edge of the cliff. One hundred feet below the turbulent sea crashed against rocks. The rain returned with a vengeance, bouncing off his hat and overcoat.

I haven't lost yet, he thought. *I have paid for these women. They are my property.*

The waves thundered as Robert stood there, his anger growing.

I need to put Denton on a bus to Brookings with instructions to find out where April parent's live. While he's doing that I'll search for Charley's car on the highway. He won't get far with a drained radiator. First things first, he thought as he got back into the passenger seat of the Lincoln,

Chapter Fifteen

April asked, "How does it work anyway?" She was holding the umbrella against the rain, coming through the gap in the car's roof.

"What do you mean?"

"The girls. I mean, how did they get here from China?" April looked in the back seat. The girls were sleeping.

The rain had lessened to a drizzle. The sun was lighting up the east.

"Well, I think it works this way. The girls were probably sold into slavery by their dissatisfied Chinese parents. Their father was probably furious because his wife didn't bear a son. So he sold the girls. Then a Japanese broker bought them. He arranged for them to be shipped to the United States. The broker got his cash from the person who sold them to Billy. Billy in turn sold them to Robert. Men like that think girls are chattel, like a couch or chair. They don't give a damn about them personally, only how they will make money."

April moved closer and rested her head on Charley's shoulder. Then she kissed his neck. "I love you, Charley."

At that moment steam started shooting up from the radiator. "What the..." Charley said. "What's wrong?"

"The engine is smoking," April said, straightening up.

Charley pulled over. "Let's go have a look." They got out and went to the front of the car. Steam was pouring out from under the hood. Charley tried to lift the hood but it was too hot. "Ow," he said. When it had cooled enough he tried again. "The radiator looks empty. Hey, look here! There are two bullet holes where the water drained out. More of Robert's work. I'll bet. What now?"

"Flag down a car?" April said.

"Okay, you stay in the car with the girls." Charley stood by the side of the road. The first, second and third cars zoomed by. After about thirty minutes a big truck pulled over. On the bed of the truck was a huge pipe, perhaps 90 inches in height and 20 feet long. The driver jumped from the cab, almost like a cat. He was a small man, hardly 5 feet tall. He had a thick brown mane and dull brown eyes.

"What's the problem, Mac?" the driver asked.

"My radiator blew up on me. I need a lift into Bandon to get a tow truck."

"That won't be necessary. I can tow you. I have chains in the cab. We can chain your car to the back of my truck. I usually have my own car on the back, but decided to leave it home on this trip. What do you think? want a tow?"

"Great. I have two sleeping passengers in the back seat. Do you think it would be safe for them to remain in my car while you tow us to town?"

"Sure. Let's get your car hooked up." He drove the big rig in front of Charley's car. Then he crawled under the Chevrolet and hooked his chains to its axle. Finally he attached the chain to a winch on his truck that lifted the car's front tires off the ground.

By the time they were set to go, April had successfully communicated to the girls what was happening. Charley and April sat up in the cab of the big truck.

"My name is Frank Brownly." The truck driver put out his small hand to Charley.

"Charley Norman. This is April Lewis."

"We really appreciate your help, Mr. Brownly," April said.

94

"Call me Frank, please." Frank pulled out a cigarette and lit up. He blew the smoke out the open window.

Charley was happy to be getting a lift, but he was also curious. "That big pipe on the back of your truck, where are you hauling it?"

"South of Gold Beach to the Pistol River construction site on the new section of Highway 101. The state is straightening the old curvy highway between Pistol River and Brookings. The ocean views from the new road will be spectacular."

Frank took a drag on his cigarette and blew the smoke out the window. Then he started the engine and shifted into first gear. He looked back through his side mirror to make sure the car was towing properly and that there was no traffic. Satisfied, he drove out onto the highway. Air whooshed in through the passenger window, helping to clear out the cigarette smoke.

"This pipe on my truck-bed is just one of many pipe sections being used to funnel creek water to the ocean," Frank explained. "Once the pipes are placed in the creeks, they fill up the canyons with dirt. The construction crews are literally leveling mountains to fill these gorges. Some of those canyons are 250 feet deep. Can you imagine that?"

"No, I can't," Charley said writing furiously on his note pad.

"It's one of the largest road projects ever undertaken by the Oregon State Highway Department. When finished this new section of highway will have the tallest bridge in Oregon, the Thomas Creek Bridge. It's 350 feet to the gorge bottom. The highway runs through Samuel Boardman State Park for ten miles. Talk about views."

Frank noticed that Charley was writing down what he was saying. "Are you a reporter?"

"Yes," Charley said. "I work for the *Oregonian* in Portland. I was sent down here to investigate this road project. What else do you know about it?"

Frank thought a moment, "Actually, the first part of the project was two years ago. The old Roosevelt Highway, used to go through

Coquille to reach Bandon. In 1960 they straightened it to bypass Coquille entirely. The mileage is shorter and the road straighter. I used to hate driving the curvy Roosevelt sections."

Soon they reached Bullards Bridge just north of Bandon.

"There's a garage, up here on the left, next to the Bandon Cheese Company. I know the owner. His work is good, with honest rates."

"Nice," April said.

Frank unhitched their car at the garage. Before Frank drove off, Charley made sure to get Frank's contact information.

The garage mechanic inspected the car. "I can start to work on this radiator now," he said. "Fortunately, I have a replacement. A stroke of luck for you folks. Come back at 5 p.m. I should have it ready."

"Any idea where we could eat lunch?" Charley asked.

"The City of Bandon is holding a fish fry on the bay. Only 75 cents for all you can eat. We're celebrating the 4th of July two days early on Sunday this year so everyone can participate. Lots of food and fun things to do. Even a pie eating contest. You might want to enter that."

With a raised eyebrow and a smile, April motioned to the girls to follow her. The foursome headed to Bandon's harbor. They found a large group of people lining up for a buffet style lunch. Community leaders from different civic organizations were busy frying fish. French fries sizzled in pans of bubbling fat. Included in the meal were big bowls of freshly made cole slaw.

Charley paid for his group. They all got in line. When they had gotten their food, Charley led them to a table. Tables and chairs filled the sidewalks and even part of the street. Boys and girls in scout uniforms served lemonade.

"Do you celebrate like this every year?" April asked a girl pouring lemonade into paper cups.

"I guess so," the girl said. "This year we have raft races, baseball games, auctions and later tonight, fireworks on the north

96

jetty." She pointed to a line of people in front of the Bandon bakery. "They're lining up for tickets to enter the pie eating contest. That's one of our most popular events." She poured April's cup and moved on.

"I'll be right back," April said. She hurried off toward the bakery. When she returned she had a red ticket in her hand.

"What's that?" Charley asked.

"I just entered you in a pie eating contest."

"April, you should have asked me first. I have never done a contest like that. What does the winner get?"

"A freshly made blueberry pie. Don't you think it would be nice for all of us to have a pie? I'll bet the girls would love some."

"Okay, okay, I'll try. But I wish I knew strategy for winning. Some people have been doing these contests for years. When does it start?"

"Twenty minutes." Then April changed the subject. She pointed with a french fry to a long, dilapidated building on a pier that extended out into the bay. "I wonder what that building was for?" Su and Ming looked too.

"I've heard about it," Charley said. "Back in the 1920s, I guess it was the largest condensed milk factory in the United States. It was three times that size back then. The Nestle Company owned it. They bought so much milk that hundred's of dairy farmers moved to Bandon. The way I understand it, Nestle closed down in 1925 because they couldn't get a good supply of fresh water."

Charley took a bite of deep-fried halibut. Then he continued.

"After the condensary closed, the building was used for many things. At one point it was even a bordello. Without the condensary the local dairy industry concentrated more on making cheese. That's probably when that cheese factory next to the garage started."

"How do you know all this?"

"I proofread an article by a *Oregonian* reporter who did a story on it."

97

"Does the cheese factory offer tours?" April asked.

"When we finish here, we'll go find out. Might be a good story there too."

They all rose at once and walked to the bakery. Charley handed his ticket to a lady. She positioned him alongside some tables full of pies. A big group of people were crowding round.

The tables stretched along the sidewalk for thirty feet, with a pie every two feet. Fifteen people had entered. The man on the end next to Charley offered his hand.

"My name is Clarence. May the best man win."

Charley shook his hand.

I'll never beat him, Charley thought. *He has an enormous mouth. I think mouth size has something to do with the strategy.*

Clarence waved to his wife and daughter in the front row. April, Su and Ming were behind them. The contestants stood in front of their pies. Charley looked down at his. The pie looked really delicious, and really big. It would be a shame to waste it.

The starter had a cap pistol. "When I shoot this pistol you will begin. Keep your hands behind your back at all times or you'll be disqualified."

Bang!

The fifteen contestants bent down and began frantically gobbling up their pies. The lady who had taken Charley's ticket was also the judge. She walked back and forth in front of the table. It was her job to declare a winner. Screams from the crowd egged on certain contestants. Clarence's wife and daughter were the most vocal. "You better win, Clarence! We want that pie."

"Faster, Daddy, faster, please faster Daddy, go Daddy."

April yelled to Charley "Hurry up, dear." The two girls yelled "Hurly up, hurly up".

Charley was eating as fast as he could. It was a blackberry pie, very good. As he gobbled the pie, bits of it stuck to his beard stubble, got up his nose and dribbled down on his sweater.

Although he was eating as fast as he could, Charley still had a quarter of his pie left when the judge declared Clarence the winner. His wife and daughter ran up to the table to hug Clarence. They collected their big blueberry pie. When Charley looked up he resembled a strange Oreo cookie-black on the bottom, white in the middle and red on top.

Blackberry pie filling stretched from one of Charley's ears to the other. His entourage were all bent over laughing. Charley didn't think it was so funny. He found a paper towel and wiped the jam from his face and sweater. Then he laughed too. "That was tasty," he admitted.

The contestants were allowed to keep what was left of their pies. With his pie in hand, Charley led the girls toward the cheese factory. Behind them new pie eating contestants filed in for another contest.

"I'll get back at you April, you just wait." They crossed Highway 101.

A doorbell tinkled as they entered the cheese factory showroom.

Chapter Sixteen

"Now, don't forget your assignment, Denton." Robert was sipping coffee from a paper cup. They were at the Coos Bay bus station. "Find out where her parents live. When you find their home, stick around for a few hours and see if you can see them. Check to see if their home has a back door. Check for dogs. When you feel like you have enough information, go to the Chetco Bridge. Hang around until I get there. In case I'm not successful in getting back my girls, we'll take April's parents hostage. Did you get your ticket?"

Denton took a swig of his coffee, and nodded. "Yes, I'm ready to go." The 10 a.m. bus was idling at the curb.

"All aboard." The bus driver smiled. "I have a schedule to keep."

"Here's a few bucks, Denton. Remember their last name is Lewis. You'll have to look up that name in the phone book to find where they live. You got that?"

"Sure, sure, you already told me that."

"Good luck, then. I'll see you at the bridge."

Denton boarded the bus.

Robert got into his white Lincoln Continental and checked his map. *Bandon is the next town south.*

The rain had cleared. The sun was nearing its peak.

Now I'll find out how Charley handles a leaking radiator. Ha, you dumb shit, what will you do now?

Forty-five minutes later the white Lincoln passed over the Bullards Bridge on the outskirts of Bandon.

Robert knew that Charley's car would need major radiator repair work. To find Charley all he had to do was to locate the garage doing the repairs. He spent about an hour looking.

How dumb of me! I passed right by the garage. How was I to know it would be a block off the main street, hidden behind Bandon's Cheese Factory?

Robert drove slowly past the garage. He could see Charley's car up on the lube rack. Robert parked his Lincoln on a side street not far from the garage, where he could view the big red garage door. Robert had lost one gun at the Tioga Hotel. But he had a spare in the glove compartment. He placed that gun into his shoulder holster. He would simply have to wait until they returned for their car.

Meanwhile Denton had already gone through Bandon, past cranberry bogs, dairies, and sheep on hillsides. The bus was approaching Langlois, many miles south of Bandon. Sitting next to him at the window was a middle-aged women knitting a child's bonnet. She wore a gingham dress with bright yellow vertical stripes.

"Where are you going?" she asked Denton.

"To Brookings," Denton said.

"Do you have business there?"

"It's personal. I don't want to talk about it."

"We have about two more hours to go. And they might even delay us at Pistol River. We might as well get to know each other."

"Why would they delay us?"

"They're building the new highway. Lots of big equipment and road work."

"So what?" Denton said, a little agitated.

Why couldn't this women shut up?

101

Finally, a little nastily he said, "Where are you going, lady?"

"I'm going home to Brookings. My husband will be waiting for me at the station. My name isn't lady, either. It's Marsha. Marsha Lewis. My daughter is a school teacher in Portland. Would you like to see her picture?"

The name rattled around in Denton's brain for a few minutes. *Marsha Lewis, Marsha Lewis, Marsha Lewis... No way*, he thought. *This couldn't be true.*

"Yes, yes, I would like to see her picture."

Marsha laid her knitting aside and reached into her big yellow purse. "I've been in Coos Bay for a physical. Both my husband and I like the doctor there. A personal friend. You know when you're my age good health is very important. What was it you were going to Brookings for?"

Even though he was sitting next to his prey, her inquisitiveness annoyed him.

I have to come up with a good reason for going to Brookings.

"My boss is an investor. He sent me down here to scout out a piece of property. He wants to build a big motel there."

"Not another investor! My husband, Grant and I are against such developments. We want our town to stay small. We've protested for years at City Hall against these big motels. We're afraid the building of the new road will really open up our city to over-development."

Marsha had already decided she didn't want to show her daughter's picture to this man. She didn't like him. He smelled like he hadn't had a bath in days, and his stubble was offensive, and his breath was foul. "Sorry, I can't find her picture." She huffed and turned to the window for air. Then she resumed her knitting.

Denton tried clumsily to restart the conversation with Mrs. Lewis. He failed miserably. She closed up like a clam. He decided he would watch her when she got off the bus. He'd see what her husband looked like and follow them to their house. If Mr. Lewis was in a car, he'd have to look up their address in the phone book.

All in all, Denton felt quite satisfied with himself. He had accomplished one part of his mission. He already had Mr. Lewis's first name. It shouldn't be hard to find their address in the phone book. He wouldn't tell Robert how easy it was.

Because the bus was on a schedule it was permitted faster routing through the construction area. It was hardly delayed at all.

The bus drove into the bus terminal. "Brookings," the driver announced. "We'll be here twenty minutes. There are food and snacks in the station. Next stop is Crescent City."

Mrs. Lewis had to nudge Denton, asleep in the aisle seat.

"Please, I have to get off here."

"Oh, yes." He quickly got up and let her out. Then he watched out the window. He saw her meet her husband Grant. They walked to their car and drove away.

Denton went inside the bus building and found a pay telephone attached to a wall. A telephone book was underneath on a ledge. The book had thick plastic covers secured by a wire cable to the wall so no one would steal it. Denton looked up the Lewis's address: 475 E. A Street.

Chapter Seventeen

"Please come in. Let me introduce myself. My name is Roger Vogt, manager of Bandon's Cheese Factory. Roger was over six feet tall, an energetic, heavy-set man who waved his arms and hands as he talked. "I'm really glad you folks stepped in. We have a new product I think you will enjoy. You will be the first to sample our new smoked cheddar cheese." Roger brought out a big plate of sliced yellow cheese. "Please, try some. Where are you folks from?"

"Portland. I'm a writer for the Portland *Oregonian*. Mmm, this is good cheese."

"Thank you. Here, let me give you two bricks of cheese to share with your office. I'd like to know what journalists think about our smoked cheddar." Roger's hands almost reached the ceiling in a dramatic flair. "Any mention of our new product in your paper would be highly appreciated. Our products can be ordered through the mail. Here are some pamphlets that tell about our business. Now let me take you through our plant." He opened a door that entered into the factory area.

In the first room a man was stirring a big vat of cheese curds. "This is what our cheese looks like before it's pressed into cheese bricks, like the ones I gave you earlier. Here, try some curds." They all sampled the white globs.

"Those smoking pots over there are how our aging cheddar is smoked. We hope it will be a big seller."

Charley and the girls followed Roger around the plant as he showed them the various processes involved in making cheese—

cooking, stirring, fermenting, pressing, aging and finally wrapping. All this time Charley was taking notes. The girls tried different types of cheese. In all it took about an hour. Charley got Roger's contact information and the group left out the back door, near the garage where Charley's car was having a new radiator installed.

The mechanic told Charley he almost had Charley's car ready. "Give me another half hour and you can drive it away. There are magazines and newspapers in the waiting room. Just make yourselves comfortable while I finish up. Are you folks staying for the fireworks this evening?"

"I would like to," April said moving a lock of hair behind her ear. She then looked at Charley's blue eyes. He pushed his glasses up the bridge of his nose,

"Let's do it." Charley led the way to the waiting room. Su and Ming followed.

As promised, the car was ready half an hour later. Charley paid for the work. After tucking the paperwork in his back pocket, Charley drove out the big front door of the garage. As he turned onto Highway 101 he noticed a few more rattles.

~~~~~

Denton stepped outside the bus terminal and found he was on the corner of Main Street and A Street. The Lewis's lived on A Street.

This will be easy, Denton thought.

So he walked east on A Street until he found the Lewis's home. It was a single-story rectangular home with a long gabled roof and attached garage. One big cedar tree stood in the front yard. The grass was turning brown. Denton noticed an alleyway in back. He walked down the alley to the back of the house. Steps led up to a screened back porch. There was no fence. There didn't appear to be any sign of a dog.

Denton decided his job was finished. He went back to town, rented a motel room, and took a nap. When he finally woke up it was past 5 p.m. "I'd better get to the bridge," he mumbled. He had to walk clear through town to find the Chetco Bridge.

In the meantime Robert had noticed Charley's car driving from the garage to Highway 101. "Hmmm," he said to himself, and started the Lincoln.

"We'll have to hide the car someplace," Charley said. "I don't want that idiot Robert messing with my car again."

"But where?"

At the north end of Bandon Charley turned west off Highway 101 onto Fillmore Drive. At that corner of First Street he noticed that the gate to the old Condensed Milk factory building was wide open.

"Robert would never find us if we parked inside that building," Charley drove out the pier. The front of the building had a opening as large as the mechanic's garage. He drove inside. "We'll stay here until dusk, then walk to the south jetty and watch the fireworks. We should be safe here."

~~~~

But Robert had carefully followed them from the garage to the big, dilapidated building on the pier. Robert parked out of sight on Riverside Drive and waited. From his vantage point he could see them inside the car. There was only one way out for them, and that was back along the pier. He wondered what they were up to.

Robert noticed a crowd of people further out on the north jetty. Something was going on out there. Then it dawned on him.

Fourth of July fireworks. That's what Charley and the girls are waiting for. They're waiting for the fireworks display. They're sitting pigeons. I can supply them with fireworks of my own.

He pushed open his door and went to the rear of his car. He unlocked the truck lid. Inside was a case with a high-powered rifle. Robert removed the gun, and closed the the trunk. He returned to his driver's seat. Resting the gun barrel on the open window's ledge, he adjusted the sights. "Ah, yes," he said. He could see Charley in the car. That's when he took aim.

Damn those girls, sit down, will you? Hold still, Charley! stop kissing April!

His finger began squeezing the trigger. A strong gust of wind pushed against the Lincoln as the shot was fired, throwing it off its trajectory. The bullet slammed into the wall of the garage—directly in front of Charley's car. Robert fired again but by this time Charley's car was in motion. Robert's bullet banged into Charley's trunk. At the same time a sea gull emptied himself in the sky, and the white milky substance whipped this way and that, in an erratic fall, splashing onto Robert's gun barrel. One strand of the slimy goo hit his forehead and began dripping down his face.

Chapter Eighteen

Charley sped over the pier to Fillmore Street and out onto the Highway 101, heading south.

"He just tried to shoot us!" April was nearly in tears. "Will this ever stop?"

"Once we're further south of Bandon we'll try to find another hiding place. We'll be more careful next time. Keep your eyes open."

As they drove south Charley kept glancing in the rearview mirror. No sign of the Lincoln. That didn't mean Robert and his cohorts weren't there. Charley had driven about twenty minutes when April spotted the turnoff to Cape Blanco.

"Shall we?"

Charley took the road that led to Oregon's western most point, the Cape Blanco lighthouse. The road turned from pavement to gravel. Suddenly there was a bang, and the car began bumping.

"We have a flat," Charley announced.

"Oh, no!" April said. Su and Ming looked frightened.

He pulled the car over on a level shoulder. "Everyone out, stretch your legs while I fix the tire." April motioned to Su and Ming to move outside. They all huddled behind Charley as he opened the trunk. Su kept Ming close to her. Dusk was settling in. Their shadows stretched across the gravel road.

From the trunk Charley took out the jack, lug wrench and spare tire. Charley levered the jack, raising the left rear axle off the ground. Then he pried off the hub cap and began removing the lugs. Then Charley heard an approaching car and looked up. A Pontiac pulled up beside them. The driver got out. He wore a dark leather jacket. His dog jumped out with him.

"Hi, can I be of any help?" He pushed back the brim of his baseball cap. He was middle aged, and thin, with a goatee and smartly curled mustache. In one hand he held a uniquely decorated cane with a metal tip and in the other hand, he held a leash tied to a black lab's collar.

"I'm almost finished here," Charlie said. "I'll tighten these last two lugs then put the flat tire in the trunk."

The lab looked at Charlie with soulful brown eyes.

"Here, boy." Charlie reached out and petted him. The dog wagged his tail. Then the dog licked the jam on Charley's sweater. Charley had to push him away. The girls petted the dog too. Ming sat on the ground and roughhoused with him.

"What's his name?" April asked.

"Rosebud," the man said pulling down his brim. "One night about four years ago he was left on our front porch. He was in a big wicker basket with a note attached to its handle. 'Please take care of our dog. We are unable to care for him. He is yours.' A rosebud was also in the basket. So that's what we decided to call him. Seems strange for a male dog, but it works. Never did find out who left him. By the way my name is Angus Hughes. I live down the hill from here. You can see my house through the trees." He pointed down the hill with his cane.

"You mean that beautiful two story Queen Anne home?" Charley said.

"Yes, that is my home. It was built by my relatives in 1898, Patrick and Jane Hughes. We've been in the dairy business ever since. We own roughly 1800 acres. Don't know how much longer my wife and I can hold out, though. It's a lot to care for. What is your name, sir? "

"Charley Norman, and these are April, Su and Ming."

"Charley Norman, I've heard that name before. Are you a journalist?"

"Yes."

"Are you the Norman who writes about the corruption in Portland, with the *Oregonian*?"

"Yes." Charley explained to Angus their situation. He added that they needed a place to hide the car and spend the night.

"I see. I think I can help you. We have an old barn down there where we can hide your car. You can spend the night in our bunkhouse. We have many beds there and tons of bedding. No one will find you. How does that sound?"

"The faster we can get down there the better. We'll leave early and try not to bother you and your wife. What is her name?"

"Ava. You'll not leave without having breakfast with us." Angus said with a sparkle in his eye. "Ava loves to cook. She'd be disappointed if you didn't stay for breakfast. She'll be delighted you folks are spending the night. She's read all your columns. Both of us are always amazed at the prostitution rings in Portland. You're a hero Charley for tackling a mob like that."

Angus leaned his cane against his leg, then twirled his mustache, "Ava was making dinner when I left. I will hurry down there and tell her we're having company. After you put your tools in the trunk, drive down to my house. I'll show you where to park and where the bunkhouse is. You won't be bothered, believe me. We seldom have company. When we do, it is a real treat for us. We have another dog at the house, a Doberman, named Betsy, who could make life miserable for anyone wanting to harm you. Betsy will stay with you in the bunkhouse. She won't let any harm come to you. I want you to get a good night's sleep. Drive down there and we'll meet at the house."

At the house Angus introduced the group to his wife, an energetic middle-aged women wearing a full-length flowered dress. Her dark hair was pinned up. She was heavy but firm. Angus unleashed Rosebud and pushed him into the house.

"Dinner will be ready in fifteen minutes. Fresh squash and greens from our garden. T-bone steaks from our cattle. Is that okay with you folks?"

"I think we can endure it," Charley said, laughing.

"Oh, and homemade sourdough rolls. Hurry up now, get settled. We'll see you back here in fifteen minutes."

About an eighth of a mile north of the house stood the dilapidated barn, with a bunk house nearby. Angus showed Charlie where to park his car inside the barn. Next Angus closed the eight-foot door. Then he locked it with a padlock. Next he led them to the bunkhouse. From a closet he removed bedding for the group.

"The shower and bathroom are at the west end there." He pointed with his cane. "I'm looking forward to you folks joining us. See you shortly." Angus limped toward his house.

When the group had showered and cleaned up they hiked the trail to the back door of the beautiful home. Ava was there to greet them. Charley and the girls caught whiffs of a fresh strawberry pie cooling on the window sill.

"This way," Ava said. "The table is all set."

Inside the house the first thing that struck Charley as unusual were the high ceilings. He'd seen mansions like this in Portland. But he'd never seen a house so grand on the Oregon Coast. Ava showed them to the dining room. A chandelier hung from the ceiling. A huge, ornate oriental rug hid most of the varnished wood floor. The walls had decorative wall paper and wood wainscoting. A tall vertical window allowed light through a lacy curtain. A candelabra was centered on a massive oak dining room table with seven matching chairs. The table was elegantly set for seven people.

Su and Ming, not used to such opulence, couldn't stop staring at everything. April tried to make them comfortable by sitting next to them. Su kept her arm around Ming. From the pass-through pantry Ava took some fresh-cut vegetables for the party to nibble on. The pies' aroma mixed with the smell of broiling steaks. Ava served the meal in large ornate pottery bowls in the center of the table. Big spoons were available to ladle out vegetables, mashed potatoes, and dark brown gravy. A large platter displayed the steaks.

Suddenly Betsy, the Doberman, barged into the room.

"Out!" was all Angus had to say. Betsy retreated to the living room with her ears back.

When everything had been set, Angus delivered a short prayer. Afterward, at the other end of the table Ava began dishing up, the clue for everyone else to dive in. Which they did.

Charley and his bunch were devilishly hungry. No one talked for a while as steak was cut, and the food vanished as if by magic. Ava kept a close watch on her guests' plates while eating a healthy portion herself. But she was burning with curiosity. When their plates were nearly empty, she couldn't keep quiet any longer.

"Mr. Norman, Angus filled me in on why you folks have ended up here. How is your battle with the mafia going?"

Charley adjusted his glasses. "Unfortunately, Portland is but one small market, in a world of prostitution. My hope is to clear up things there. It will settle an old score for me and make life much easier for April."

"It's a sad commentary on our society," Angus said. With his fingers he pulled slightly on his goatee. "We must educate our youth that there is more to life then succumbing to the temptations of money. Even the criminal loses in the end. In self respect, and no doubt jail time."

"We are lucky Mr. Norman," Ava said. "We live far from the big city culture. We produce most of our needs on our farm. It is not an easy life, but it is personally rewarding and allows us to live by our religious beliefs. We value faith and character."

"Sometimes I get the feeling," April said, "that the larger the city, the more corruption it has and the harder it is to keep law and order."

"I couldn't agree more," Angus said.

In the front room, Betsy's ears suddenly flipped up. She growled deeply, and raced to the big front window. She stretched up full length with her claws on the window, barking. Angus got to the window just in time to see the taillights of a white Lincoln pulling out of his driveway.

"Looks like some of your friends, Charley," Angus said, returning to the table. "They won't be back."

Su put her arm around Ming's shoulder and smiled at her. Su had sensed the moment of danger. Her tenderness toward her little sister brought a tear to Ava's eye.

"Why not let your young friends spend the night upstairs?" Ava said. "We have a big guest room, with a four-poster bed, lace curtains, and beautiful artwork, better then any four-star hotel. It's all made up. I have a feeling they might enjoy it."

"I think they would!" April said.

After dinner April and Ava led the girls upstairs to a gorgeous room with Persian carpets and floral wall paper. When the two girls understood that this room was where they would spend the night, their mouths dropped open.

When they were settled and tucked in bed, April and Ava returned to the dining room.

"Don't worry about cleaning up. Angus and I will take care of everything. You two go get some sleep. You're safe here for the night."

Charley and April expressed their thanks. Then they walked hand-in-hand down the hill to the bunkhouse. Betsy followed.

Charley flipped on the light as they entered. They were very tired. They picked out two single beds that were side by side. Once they had adjusted their gear, they turned back the covers to their beds. Then, April turned off the lights. Betsy lay in her own little bed by the door.

Charley woke up three hours later. Moonlight brightened the room. *I wonder if that really was Robert in Angus' driveway last night. If I don't stop him, he'll chase after us forever. I need to find a way to put Robert behind bars, and soon.*

"Are you awake?" April said.

"Yes."

"I know what you're thinking about. Together we are strong, Charley. Robert doesn't have a chance. Su and Ming are safe for the night. We're safe here, too. The safest I've felt in a long time."

"I know what you mean," Charley said. "I just want you to know, no matter what happens, I have so much respect for you. I hope I don't let you down."

"Charley, you won't. You've already proven your character to me. Don't worry about Robert tonight, Charley. He wins the battle if you hate him too much. I feel you and I have a special bond. It's stronger then Robert. I'm so proud of what we're doing." April got out of bed. The moonlight showed through her thin negligee.

"Wow! Where did you get an outfit like that?" Charley asked.

April put her finger to his lips. "Tonight is our night."

~~~~

After breakfast Charley's team piled into his car and drove out to Highway 101. Once again Charley turned right toward Brookings. The wind seemed to be increasing. April looked back at the girls. They were smiling with their hair fluttering in the wind. They seemed okay. Ming was cuddled next to her big sister. The day promised sunshine and wind.

~~~~

The unexpected splatter of sea gull excrement on the barrel of Robert's gun caused him to jump. His shot went wild. "Damn that bird!" Robert cleaned off his face and gun with his handkerchief. The Chevrolet was already just a red blur, speeding for the highway.

Almost, he thought. *All I can do now is tail them. I'm getting tired of this. What I need to do is finish off, Charley and April. Then retrieve my property. It's really quite simple. They aren't even armed. They should be easy prey.*

Robert drove south on Highway 101, frustrated, fuming like an overheated steam engine. He had let his dark beard grow.

Now it stuck out like pins in a pin cushion. In Portland, he had always been well groomed, but April and Charley were affecting everything in his life these days.

Robert knew that Charley's group was ahead of him, but he wanted to get to Brookings first. Driving south from Bandon he had already wasted a couple of hours checking out a side road into Cape Blanco State Park without spotting Charley's red Chevrolet. He'd even been chased away from an old mansion by a barking Doberman.

Now, back on Highway 101, he had time to collect his thoughts.

That dumb shit Denton better have found out where April's parent's live. That's my ace in the hole. If I can take the Lewises hostage then I can trade them for my Asian girls. Then kill the lot of them, maybe even Denton. The hell with them all. I should have killed Charley years ago. I should have killed April when I had the chance, too. When I get my girls I can return to the Vancouver operation. When this is over it will send a message to the Oregonian *that if you mess with Robert Taylor, there are real consequences.* Robert rubbed his stubble.

As he was thinking, an ocean fog bank rolled in. He had to slow down because he could only see a few feet in front of him. He turned on his headlights, but that actually blinded him worse. He drove slowly all the way to the town of Port Orford, where he stopped and rented a motel room. He figured that he would leave early the next morning and make a beeline for Brookings.

One way or another, Robert reasoned, *I will get my property back.*

Chapter Nineteen

Charley was in deep thought, driving to Port Orford. He didn't know that Robert had already left ahead of him. So, he remained vigilant.

Charley, April and the Chinese girls were in good spirits, thanks to the Hughes' hospitality. Their warm "goodbyes," their "please be safe," their "we want to read more of your articles," their smiles to the children, all left Charley and April with a warm glow.

Not only that, Charley thought, *From now on I know that April and I are in this together, solidly. Of course, I've known that all along. But now there is a deeper tie. There is a serious commitment, tied by the night's intimacy.*

But Charley's thoughts quickly turned to Robert.

I have to get more evidence on him. When we get him into court we cannot afford to lose. That's the whole point now, isn't it? We're going to have to take some chances. Robert initiated this terror on the coast. By now he's desperate enough that he might make a mistake, a big mistake that will lead to his arrest.

In Port Orford they suddenly came to a sweeping view of the Pacific Ocean.

"Let's drive to Port Orford's famous dry dock," April said. "I'm sure the girls will enjoy seeing boats being lowered into the sea. When a boat wants to go fishing or crabbing it is lifted by cranes and swung out over the ocean. Then it's lowered right into the Pacific. Want to see it?" She looked back at the girls and smiled.

"I do," Charley said. "I'll keep a lookout while we are out there."

Charley took the road off Highway 101 to the Port Orford dock. They parked at the end of the dock. Big waves crashed nearby. Sea gulls, buffeted by the wind, hung in the air like toy balsa wood gliders. A cormorant posed on a rocky outcrop.

They all got out of Charley's car. The wind made it hard to close the car doors. They walked along the edge of the dock looking down at the ocean. Su peered down into a fishing boat, far enough below the dock that it looked like a toy doll house. The vessel rolled in the sea as fishermen readied huge boxes of crabs. Some of the boxes had already been hoisted to the dock. There, men in white coveralls inspected and counted the crabs. The girls had big smiles on their faces.

"My father used to take me fishing here." April talked over the wind, holding her dress from flying up. "I don't think he fishes anymore. I used to really enjoy our outings. We'd catch cod and black rockfish. We didn't go out far. He liked the idea that there was no bar to cross to get to a good fishing area. Mother made us a picnic lunch. She never came, didn't like being out on the water, made her sea sick. But when we got home with the fish, she'd fry them in her special way. Then she'd combine the fish with herbed rice and vegetables from her garden. I'll never forget those days."

She looked back at the girls, their hair flying loose. Ming pointed to a boat approaching the dock.

Another big crane was getting ready to hoist it out of the sea. It took a while to get all the ropes and hooks tied to the boat. Then the crane lifted it out of the water, and gently lowered it onto a boat trailer. All around the dock were bright yellow cranes and boats of all sizes, colors and shapes.

Once back on the highway they drove alongside the Pacific Ocean with ocean views to match any photo spread in *Look* magazine. They passed by Humbug Mountain and Arizona Beach. Roadside signs started popping up advertising the Prehistoric Gardens.

"Charley, we have to stop at the Prehistoric Gardens. The owner has sculpted replicas of prehistoric monsters. His replicas of dinosaurs are suppose to be pretty accurate. You might interview the owner for a story."

"Sure, we'll stop there."

"We have a flying pteranodon with a wing span of 27 feet," the garden host said. "The walk through our garden is only about thirty minutes and features dinosaurs that lived over 70 million years ago. Our main attraction is the brachiosaurus, which stands 46 feet tall. Then there is the prehistoric forest. The wind won't bother anything. You're perfectly safe while you're in the garden. Take your time and enjoy. "

Charley said he'd keep watch outside while the girls did the tour.

~~~~

A few hours prior to April and Charley's arrival, Robert had already driven by the Prehistoric Gardens. He was so intent on getting to Brookings he hardly noticed Sisters Rocks, Nesika Beach, Otter Point, and the other viewpoints north of the Rogue River.

The wind shoved at Robert's Lincoln as he entered the north end of the bridge into Gold Beach. Robert fantasized shooting at Charley from one of the bridge's decorative pylons.

He rolled through Gold Beach in no time. Robert grew anxious, now that Brookings was only about thirty miles away. But after another ten miles his smooth sailing came to an abrupt halt. Highway construction signs warned of delays. At the Carpentersville turnoff he had to stop behind a long line of cars. Heavy equipment was moving south in the opposite lane. A man from the work crew walked along the line alerting each parked car about the delay.

"It'll be about a 30 minute wait while we move through equipment and materials for the new Thomas Creek Bridge. The old highway is still open and you'll be able to use it shortly. Thanks for your patience."

The workman with an orange hard hat moved to the next car. The wind began ratcheting up.

Maybe fifty miles an hour, Robert thought. Loose shrubbery and tree limbs were blowing across the road and banging into cars.

The workman switched his sign from "Stop" to "Slow." The cars began moving, picking up speed.

As Robert turned east on the Carpentersville road he noticed the new highway shooting south along the ocean's edge. He wished he could drive that way.

As he drove east the wind increased still more. He noticed that the trees were really taking a beating. Some of the cedars bent over so far they looked like old women loaded down with bags of groceries. As the road curved south and climbed, Robert noticed thicker groves of trees. On his right was a steep dropoff. As he rounded one curve a huge semi truck, fighting the wind, almost shoved Robert's car off the road. The truck was weaving all over the place and nearly collided with a car behind Robert. The further south he drove the denser the forest became. Big lumber trucks began speeding past him. He decided to pull over.

Robert got out of the car and stood at the cliff's edge. He could still see the ocean, and the gorge where the men were working on the new bridge. He grabbed his binoculars from the glove compartment. He was surprised to see that the finished highway stopped at either side of the gorge. The bridge would connect the two roads. On closer observation Robert could see that the workmen were packing up. They were calling it a day because of the wind.

The Thomas Creek gorge was a "V" shaped funnel that rose from the ocean and flattened out as it climbed into the mountains where Robert was standing. Wind rushed up at him so hard he had to step back to remain standing. He heard a tree below him crack and snap, sending the top smashing to the ground. The top boughs of it landed nearly at Robert's feet. As he stepped back another Douglas fir next to him swayed in an enormous gust of wind, up-ending its roots, and toppled to the ground. With an ear shattering crunch, the fir landed on top of Robert's car. It had all happened so fast. The tree had not only totaled Robert's car, it had blocked the highway too.

Robert managed to open the passenger side door. He grabbed his rifle and wrapped it in a coat to hide it. He waited half an hour in the ruin of his car before workmen arrived with chainsaws. A big truck with a winch pulled the tree off his car and cleared the road enough to open one lane of traffic. Robert's car was obviously beyond repair.

Robert asked one of the workmen if he could get a lift into Brookings. The truck driver happened to be going that way so he agreed to help Robert. He let Robert out at the Brookings bus station. From there, Robert walked to the Chetco Bridge. Denton was sitting on a folding chair, staring at the river below.

"We have to act fast," Robert said. "Charley and friends are on their way here. Do you know where the Lewises live?"

"Sure thing, boss," Denton said. "It was hard work but I got their address. I'll take you to my motel room. I have a map there. We can plan our attack. Where's your car?"

"Totaled by a falling Douglas fir." I'll tell you on the way. Let's move."

~~~~

April and the girls had been in the Prehistoric Gardens during the wind storm. It had been great fun following the tracks of dinosaurs along a path that criss-crossed a stream on little bridges. The dinosaurs hid among the ferns, and fir trees. The girl's favorite dinosaur was the triceratops. It was a massive animal like a hippopotamus but had two horns that jutted out of its forehead.

Charley joined the group in the gift shop. April bought two coloring books and crayons for the girls. Charley gathered brochures. Then the foursome returned to Charley's car. The wind had abated by this time.

"The great Rogue River is straight ahead," Charley said. He started his car and drove out onto the highway. They all were glad that the weather had cleared up, although the gap in the convertible's roof still let in a noisy rush of wind.

They maintained a steady pace enjoying rock-studded ocean views leading into the city of Gold Beach. After crossing the Rogue River Charley stopped at a little cafe at the south end of town.

"We don't serve Japanese," the waitress said.

"They're Chinese," Charley said.

"It doesn't matter."

"Let's find another place," April said. A nearby market sold them bread, lunch meats and Cokes. They ate at a picnic table at a wayside overlook. After lunch Su and Ming went down to the beach to build a castle.

April frowned looking out at the great blue undulating carpet of sea. "Will people ever get over their racism?"

"It takes a while," Charley said. "Generations, unfortunately."

"I just don't understand it. We're all the same. Arms, legs, brains, passions, needs. Aren't we all the same, Charley?"

"I think so."

"Maybe someday, people will find a way to overcome their old prejudices."

"I don't know," Charley said. "But we should get going."

Charley called the girls. They were having so much fun they didn't want to leave their sand castle. The tide was already lapping at the moat. Reluctantly Su and Ming started walking back to the car. Meanwhile a wave flattened their castle.

The Carpentersville road leading east off Highway 101 was now fully open. Once the fallen trees had been removed, traffic was flowing again. At the turnoff, Charley pulled over to the west side of the road in a construction parking area. A workman wearing a yellow hard hat came over to the car.

"Hey buddy. You have to take the Carpentersville road to get to Brookings. This route is still under construction."

"I'm a reporter with the *Oregonian* newspaper. I would like to get some photographs of the work you guys are doing here. Who do I talk to about that?"

"I can handle that. I'm the supervisor of the northern section. What do you need?"

"To drive to the bridge construction site and back. Would that be possible?"

"Sure, I'll lead you in my pickup truck." He said pointing to an orange truck. "Once we get to the bridge I have to stay there, though. You'd have to drive back alone. Are you okay with that?"

"Yes."

"One thing to notice on the way to the bridge are all the scenic turnouts. Spectacular views at each site. You'll see."

"Okay," Charley said.

Charley got out of the car and walked with the supervisor to his pickup. On the way, Charley asked, "what type of bridge are you building at Thomas Creek?"

"A continuous deck truss, 956 feet long. Two steel towers hold it up. The roadbed is thirty feet wide. The bridge will be the tallest in Oregon at 345 feet. One joker already jumped off the deck."

"Did he survive?"

"Are you kidding me? No way. We aren't publicizing the guy's name, so this is strictly between you and me. We don't want copycats."

"No problem. I'll respect that."

Charley furiously wrote down answers to questions in his notebook. When the supervisor got in his truck Charley ran back to the Chevrolet.

The supervisor drove south along the new road. Charley followed. When they reached the bridge construction area, Charley had April take photographs. The bridge was being built from south to north. The finished part of the bridge was extended well beyond its vertical steel tower support and hung suspended above the deep gorge. When Charley was finished taking notes he turned his car around. Driving back he stopped at some of the overlooks, and had April take pictures of Arch Rock and the Natural Bridge.

Charley had relaxed somewhat knowing that Robert could not follow them onto a road under construction. But then they drove back to the Carpentersville turnoff and began the journey to Brookings over the curvy inland road.

Suddenly Charley was on high alert, watching for Robert's white Lincoln. The only white car he saw was was a wreck on the shoulder, but it was smashed so badly he couldn't tell what make it was.

Chapter Twenty

In the motel room, Robert and Denton were looking over Denton's town map. The Lewis's home was circled in ink.

"Their home isn't far from here," Denton said. "We can be there in ten minutes, maybe sooner. It's at 475 E. A street, right there. "

"I see it."

"There's also an alley access to the back of their house," Denton added.

"Any sign of dogs?"

"No."

Robert thought a moment. "Okay here's what we'll do. While I knock at the front door you enter by the back. I'll keep them busy while you sneak up from behind with your revolver. Then we tie them up. April will probably call before she brings over her group. When she does we'll set up the conditions for the trade."

"Then what, boss?"

"I'm not sure. We'll have to see how things work out. Let's go."

They began their walk east on A street. When they got to the 400 block, Robert motioned Denton to the alley. Robert waited a short time, giving Denton plenty of time to get set up at the rear of the Lewis house.

Robert walked to the front door and rang the bell. Mr. Lewis answered the door. He stood six feet tall in his brown bathrobe and slippers. His salt-and-pepper hair was uncombed. His nose resembled a red cherry, and it dripped although he blew it from time to time.

"I have some bad news for you, sir. It's about your daughter, April."

"What! Is she all right?"

"Could I come inside, Mr. Lewis?"

Grant Lewis frowned, but he held the door open for Robert.

Marsha came running into the living room. "What is it Grant?"

Grant sneezed. He used a tissue to blow his nose. "This man says he has some information about April. Excuse me, but I haven't been feeling well lately. Please sit down."

Robert sat on a red love seat while the Lewises sat on a brown couch facing him. Before Robert could speak they heard a noise at the back door.

"I'll go see what that is," Marsha said. But before she could stand up she saw Robert's revolver pointing at her.

"What on earth?"

"Stay seated." Robert commanded. "That will be Denton. Come on in, Denton."

When Denton entered the room Marsha cried out in surprise."You!"

"Yup," Denton said. He explained to Robert about meeting Mrs. Lewis on the bus.

"I see," Robert said. "Well, I don't think the Lewises will cause us any trouble. Do you have some rope, Mr. Lewis?"

"In the garage."

"Denton, go find the rope."

"What's this all about?" Grant demanded. Where's my daughter?"

"Your daughter and her boyfriend Charley have some property that belongs to me, and I want it back."

Marsha shook her head. "I told you, Grant. April should never gotten mixed up with that reporter."

"Oh, hush." Grant looked to Robert. "So why are you barging in here with guns?"

"I plan to trade you folks to Charley for my property. A very simple trade. I'd be careful if I were you, if you want your daughter back alive."

When Denton returned with the cord, Robert ordered the Lewises to sit in dining room chairs. Then Denton secured them to the chairs with the rope.

"Where is my daughter?" Grant asked, sneezing.

"She'll be here soon." Robert kept his gun pointed at Marsha. "Where are the keys to your car.?"

"In my pants pocket," Grant said. "My pants are on the bed in my bedroom."

"Denton come with me while I get the keys." When they were alone in the bedroom Robert said, "I'm going to take their car to the new highway and follow it to the bridge that's under construction. I'm thinking that will be a quiet place to make the trade. But I need to look it over beforehand. You stay here with the Lewises. If April calls tell her we have her parents tied up. If she wants them to stay alive have her call back in an hour. Tell her not to come here. If she does, shoot her parents. Now go back to the living room and stay there until I get back."

"Sure. Let me check Grant's wallet first. He won't need money anymore."

In the garage Robert found the Lewis' blue 1952 Chevrolet coupe. Robert opened the garage door, looked around, then drove the car out. With the car idling in the driveway, he closed the garage door.

He hadn't driven a stick shift for a while. It jumped and rocked as he put the car in gear. But once he was on the road, shifting became easier. Robert drove to the new highway north of Brookings. He drove around the "road-closed" signs and followed the newly paved road as it wove through Samuel Boardman State Park. Finally he arrived at the southern side of the Bridge construction area. The construction crew had left because of the heavy winds.

This will work out perfect, Robert thought. *The place is deserted.*

He also noted the wooden barricades that blocked the entrance to the unfinished bridge. The deck of the bridge jutted out over empty space. This was what he had come to find out. The second part of his plan was starting to take shape in his mind.

Robert drove back to Brookings and parked the car in the Lewis' driveway. As he entered the front door, he heard Grant sneezing. The Lewises sat quietly, scared. Denton had slugged Grant and slapped Marsha a few times. Their faces were red and bruised. A drop hung on Grant's nose.

"Did April call?"

"No, boss."

"We'll wait until she does. It shouldn't be long now."

Chapter Twenty-One

Charley was almost to Brookings when a flagger stopped their car. The flagger came up to Charley's window.

"It shouldn't be long. We have some logging equipment blocking the road up ahead." He gave Charley's car a funny look. Sir, your car is in pretty bad shape.

"Yes, I'm aware of that."

Half an hour later they finally rattled into Brookings.

"I'd better call first before we barge in," April said. "Do you have a dime?"

"Yes. There's a phone booth," Charley said.

Inside the booth April dropped the coin in the slot, then dialed her parents' number. Robert answered.

"Who's this?" April demanded.

"You know who it is. I'm here with your parents. They are inconvenienced right now. You understand, of course, April. I want my property back. Don't come here or call the police. If you do, I'll shoot these nice people. see? Now put Charley on the phone."

Charley saw April crying. She motioned for him to come quickly. He went to the booth and opened the accordion door.

"It's Robert!" April sobbed. "He has my parents. He wants to talk to you."

Charley took the phone. "This is Charley."

"So we talk again, Mr. Norman."

"What do you want?"

"Nothing complicated. I just want to exchange April's parents for the Chinese girls."

"Just a minute." Charley let the phone dangle on the cord as he and April stepped out of the booth.

"He wants to trade your parents for the girls."

April's hand flew to her mouth. "That bastard. I want to talk to my parents." They returned to the booth.

"April wants to talk to her parents."

Robert shoved the phone under Grant's mouth. "Say something."

"They're sharks, devils...."

"That's enough." Robert grabbed the phone back and slugged Grant.

"No!! Stop hitting my father."

Charley took the phone. "Okay, we believe you. They're alive."

"Now you're talking. I'll meet you in an hour at the south end of the new Thomas Creek Bridge. No one's there. It's deserted. Don't bring anyone with you, or April's parents are dead. You don't want that, do you? One hour!"

"Okay. One hour."

"What happened?" April asked.

"We have to meet Robert in one hour at the south end of the new bridge. That's where he wants to make the trade. That would give us time to call the police and work out a trap."

April shook her head. "No, too risky. Robert wouldn't hesitate to shoot my parents if anything seemed wrong."

"But we can't just turn over Su and Ming! You know what he'll do with them."

April was still shaking her head. "Making the trade will buy us time. Once my parents are safe we can go to the police and work on getting the girls back."

Charley sighed. "You're right, of course.

~~~~

Denton and Robert huddled in the kitchen. "We have to put the Lewises in the back seat of the coupe. I want to get to the construction site before Charley and the girls."

They went back into the living room and untied the Lewises. Once everyone was in Grant's car, Denton drove while Robert kept a gun pointed at the older couple.

"One false move out of either of you and Mrs. Lewis gets the first bullet."

Thirty minutes later they motored onto the construction site beside the unfinished bridge.

"Drive up to the cliff edge on the ocean side, on the other side of that big bulldozer. We don't want Charley to see Grant's car." Robert said.

"Okay, boss." They got out and were standing by the side of the car. Denton kept an eye on the Lewises.

"Now," said Robert, "I want you to tie and gag them."

While Denton worked, Robert lit up a cigarette. The smoke mingled with the light fog. With Robert's other hand he pulled out his gun. Then he carefully put on the silencer. When Denton had finished tying the Lewises, Robert said, "I want you to hide behind those trees just south of the clearing. When I give the order, sneak up behind Charley's car." Robert threw his cigarette on the ground.

"Sure, boss."

Denton turned toward the trees. Robert fired two shots in his back. Denton collapsed. Robert removed the silencer, reloaded his gun, and put it back in the holster. Then, Robert dragged Denton's body to the cliff edge, and threw him in the gorge. Next Robert checked to make sure the Lewises were secure.

I have to check out the bridge now. He squeezed around the barricade and jogged out to the end of the cantilevered bridge.

While Robert was on the bridge, Charley was driving his Chevrolet toward the construction site. Charley parked about fifty yards from the bridge barricade. They could see Robert through the light fog, walking toward them. Robert walked around the barricade.

"I'll go make arrangements." Charley said. "You stay in the car."

But when Charley got out of the car, April got out too.

"I told you to stay in the car," Charley said gruffly. He had never spoken to April like that before. "Go back and keep watch over the girls."

"No! These are my parents. I want to know whats going on. We'll go together."

"Let's go."

Robert waited at the barricade, until Charley and April were about five feet from him.

"That's far enough."

"Where are my parents?" April demanded.

Robert leveled his gun at Charley and shot him in the gut. Charley crumpled to his knees, his arms covering his stomach, then falling on his side. April instinctively followed Charley to the ground with her arms around him. Robert smacked her alongside her head with his gun. She fell away next to Charley, dazed.

From the back seat of Charley's car, Su heard the shot and saw Charley fall to the ground. It was a defining moment for her. She pulled her sister out of the car and sat her on the ground.

Su watched as Robert dragged Charley's body around the barricade to the end of the bridge.

"We haven"t much time." Su told her sister in Chinese.

Ming sat on the ground sobbing. "Listen, dearest. I love you as if you were my own child. Now is your chance for a normal life. You must take it. I am giving it to you."

Su looked down at Ming, tears dripping down her red cheeks. "Our own parents sold us into slavery. I will not let you be a slave. You are here in a free country. Stay with these people. They will help you. Now, my dearest sister, goodbye." Su bent down and kissed her sister tenderly on the forehead. Do not forget me, little one."

Robert was laughing as he pushed Charley off the bridge. He yelled, "Let's see you write about me now. You should have listened to your editor when he said your life wasn't worth a plug of tobacco. My hired men had your editor's office bugged. I knew what you were up to before you did. Ha, Charley! Goodbye, You fool."

~~~~~

Su had never felt so determined. Even though she didn't understand English, she knew what was happening. She understood that both her and Ming had been sold into the slavery of prostitution, a life of unbelievable hardship and horror. Now she had a chance to save her sister. Robert Taylor, the man who had hit her, sending her sprawling across a ballroom floor, and the man who had just pushed Charley off the bridge was the evil that had to be eradicated. Now was Su's time to act.

Su climbed into the driver's seat of Charley's car. She had seen how Charley started the engine. She started it. Su shifted the gear lever into drive.

Su put her foot on the gas pedal, pushing it to the floorboard. The car's tires spun, shooting gravel out behind. The car raced forward like a missile.

A reviving April had seen Charley thrown into the gorge. Now she watched as the Chevrolet zoomed toward the barricade. Su was driving. "Su stop!" April shouted.

In disbelief April watched as the car smashed through it, splintering it to bits. One big piece stuck in the radiator like a lance. The car looked like a unicorn, head down, and barreling toward Robert.

Robert was still laughing when he heard a roar behind him, and the sound of splintering wood as if some giant earth moving machine were headed toward him. When he turned around he saw a red car speeding at him with a splintered board jutting from the radiator. Robert didn't have time to jump out of the way. The pole pierced his body, skewering him like a matador gored by a mad bull. Robert's body squirmed in agony. His chilling scream echoed in the gorge. The car, Taylor, and Su hurtled out into space like a rocket, and then down into the gorge, crashing in a fiery explosion.

Chapter Twenty-Two

April sobbed. She knew Charley was dead. He'd been shot and pushed off the bridge. She had witnessed the death of Su and Robert. With Charley gone, April felt her life was shattered forever.

Through her tears April heard a muffled, banging noise. Looking up, she saw the front grill of her folk's car parked on the other side of a bulldozer. Her parents were banging their heads on the car window. April rushed to them. She opened the door. First she pulled the gags from their mouths. Grant had almost suffocated because of his flu. She pulled a pocket knife from her purse and cut their ropes. They all hugged.

Meanwhile April noticed Ming. The girl was sobbing as she walked out to the bridge. April was a little afraid of what the girl might see or do at the edge of the gorge. So she went to Ming and took her hand. She led Ming back to the car. April's parents hugged Ming as if she were a family member.

Thinking of Charley, April, started crying again. Her parents were crying because their daughter was alive. Eventually they all talked about what they should do next. They decided the first step was to drive to town to notify the police. They offered the back seat to Ming. Marsha Lewis climbed in beside her. Grant got in the driver's seat. April was just getting in when a truck drove into the construction site, raising dust. The truck stopped beside them.

"What's going on here?" the burly driver asked.

April tried to explain as best she could, but she became distraught and cried some more. Grant put his arm around her. The truck driver waited for April to calm down. Then he listened to her story.

"I see," the man said. "I'm the watchman for the road and bridge. Did you say someone was pushed off the bridge?"

"Yes, my fiancé,"

"Last week" the man said, "a man committed suicide by jumping off our bridge. My company decided not to tell the newspapers about the incident. Oh, we notified the man's relatives, of course, but my boss was afraid if publicity got out, someone might try to copy him. Two days ago my boss tied a net under the bridge so no one would jump off again."

"You hear that, April?" Grant said, "Charley might be at the bottom of that net. He might be alive!"

April clapped her hand to her mouth. "Quick! Let's go see!" She ran to the bridge, followed by the workman and Grant. Fearfully at the edge of the deck she leaned over and looked down. Charley's body was there! But was he alive? "Charley!" April called. He didn't move. April began crying again. The workman and Grant looked down and saw the body too.

"I'll climb down," the workman said.

"He's got a real good chance of being alive, honey," Grant told his daughter. "And to think just two days ago there wasn't a net. It's still hard to see the netting because of the fog."

The workman clambered down hand over hand to where Charley lay. "He's breathing," the guard shouted. "He's lost a lot of blood. We need to get this man to the hospital." The stocky workman carefully hefted Charley onto his broad shoulder and climbed up the net to the deck. Both April and Grant helped lift Charley onto the bridge.

"We can put him in the passenger seat of my truck. The seat adjusts way back and will allow us to get him to the emergency room faster than waiting for an ambulance. I'll also call the police pronto." They all helped carry Charley to the rig.

On the way to his rig the workman said, "I'm afraid you folks should wait here until the police arrive. They'll want to get statements from you about the incident and what happened. I wouldn't touch or move anything. Then you can go to the emergency room at the Brookings hospital to see how this guy is doing. What's his name, anyway?"

"Charley," April managed to say still fighting tears. "Charley Norman."

The workman drove off kicking up gravel. Fifteen minutes later a police car arrived. After what seemed like ages, with all the questions, April, Ming and her parents were finally allowed to go. They headed straight for the Brookings hospital.

They found Charley in a private room. His mid-section was wrapped with gauze and tape. He lay unconscious in a bed. April stood nearby with her arm around Ming. Ming clung to April as if she were Su, her lost sister.

"Dad, take mother home. You both need to rest. Dad, you go to bed and take care of your flu. I don't want you in the hospital too.

"The doctor said Charley's vital signs are stable. Charley was very lucky. The bullet went clear through on his left side, below the kidney and stomach. It missed his bones and even missed his intestines. The bullet severed a few blood vessels and that was all. He might be in shock though. We won't know until he wakes up. I'll call you as soon as I find out."

As Grant sneezed his way out of the room, April and Ming sat in chairs by Charley's bed. April kept whispering loving words in Charley's ear.

"I promise never to enter you in another pie contest. Yes, I accept your proposal to marry. We'll get married right here in Brookings. Right here in this hospital room, if you want. My parents and Ming will be present."

Charley's eyelids opened. "Get the minister," he said, grinning.

"You tease! You've been awake the whole time." She laughed, then kissed him.

Charley's first phone call was to his editor. He told Bruce that the leader of the prostitution ring had died a gruesome death.

"A deserving death," Bruce said. "The Portland police closed down Robert's operations here in Portland. Because he was gone his pimps became careless. They blabbed to Washington authorities, so now Robert's Washington operations are closed too.

"I hope you feel some vindication. Thanks for your work, Charley. When will you be healthy enough to return to work?"

"The doctors say a couple of weeks. Tomorrow April and I are getting married right here in this hospital room. We're planning on adopting Ming."

"Take an extra week for your honeymoon. I look forward to your return when everything is settled. Bye for now."

The very next morning in the hospital room the marriage ritual took place. The security guard who had carried Charley up from the net was the best man. Ming was the flower girl. April's best friend was the bridesmaid. Grant gave away the bride.

When Charley was well enough he was sent home to stay with his new in-laws. Grant drove him home. On the way he told Charley that April had decided to open a home in Portland for abused women.

"I told her I would donate money for the first year's operation."

When Grant drove Charley up to the front of his home, Charley's eyes almost popped out of his head. Sitting in the driveway of the Lewis home was a brand new red, two-door Bel Air Chevrolet.

"A wedding gift," Grant said. "Take good care of it—and my daughter."

Charley smiled. "I promise I'll do better than I did on my last trip along the Oregon Coast."

THE END

Acknowledgments

This story could not have been written without the help of William L. Sullivan. He has authored numerous books on hiking in Oregon, history of Oregon, and many novels.

Through his editorial skills and collaboration on the details of my story, a novel was born. Although the story was my idea from beginning to end, it was Sullivan's edits that helped bring the people and scenes to life.

In addition, and no less important to the production of this book, is Pat Edwards, who designed the covers, formatted the text, and helped in the editing.

Laura Wilt from the Department of Transportation archives helped me in getting the cover photographs and 1959 Oregon map.

Books by Joe R. Blakely

Oregon History

- *The Drain Black Sox of Oregon vs. The Alpine Cowboys of Texas*
- *Oswald West—Governor of Oregon 1911-1915*
- *Lifting Oregon Out Of The Mud*
- *Building Oregon's Coast Highway—1936-1966*
- *The Bellfountain Giant Killer*
- *The Tall Firs*
- *Eugene's Civic Stadium*
- *Rebellion, Murder, and a Pulitzer Prize*

Novels

- *Kidnapped—On Oregon's Coast Highway-1926*
- *The Heirloom—Bandon*
- *Crisis in Greenville*
- *Bigfoot and the Ancient Forest*
- *Deady Hall—A Ghostly Encounter*

About the Author

Joe Blakely lives with his wife, Saundra Miles in Eugene, Oregon. He has one son, Justin, and a stepson, Jonathan Baker. Mr. Blakely earned a degree in history from San Diego State College—while in college he excelled in the writing of history term papers.

Mr. Blakely retired from the office of public safety at the University of Oregon in 1999. After retirement he decided to write about Oregon history.

With the addition of this book, Mr. Blakely has written twelve books—eight are histories about Oregon. Mr. Blakely says his best work is his biography of Oswald West, Oregon's rascally governor who wrote legislation in 1913 to set aside Oregon's beaches as a highway, thereby providing public access. His two Highway 101 coast books, *Lifting Oregon Out of the Mud: Building the Oregon Coast Highway* (2006) and *Building Oregon's Coast Highway 1936-1966: Straightening Curves and Uncorking Bottlenecks* (2014) on building the coast highway, have been most popular.

To contact Joe Blakely, you can write him at
PO Box 51561, Eugene, Oregon 97405
https://joeblakelyauthor.wordpress.com/

Groundwaters Publishing, LLC
P.O. Box 50
Lorane, OR 97451
http://groundwaterspublishing.com

Made in the USA
Monee, IL
23 September 2023